ALL THE FUTURES THAT NEVER HAPPENED

All the Futures That Never Happened

Jim Stallings

First published by Oceaniacom Press 2025
A division under Oceaniacom Pty Ltd.
www.oceaniacom.com

All the Futures That Never Happened

ISBN (Print): 978-1-923113-16-9
ISBN (Ebook): 978-1-923113-17-6

Edited by Jim Stallings and Tim Humphries
Cover art by Hernán González
Cover layout by Alethea Van Holland

For shards and withers alike.
- Jim

Contents

Trigger Warnings:
This piece of fiction depicts scenes that some readers may find dis-
turbing, including illness, pre-modern medical practices, abuse,
self harm, and discriminatory behavior.
Reader discretion is advised.

THE ROAD

Escher hummed. The soles of his tattered shoes scuffed the gravel road before him as if synched with an unseen metronome. Through his many travels he had learned long ago how to smooth his voice. He sounded native to anywhere, naive to nowhere—tuned to the rhythm of foreign tongues. But Romani language is woven by music, notes like whispers that only intended ears are meant to know. So Escher hummed to himself furtive melodies from lands you and I will never fully know the day he arrived in Pathyem.

He had begun this journey with his godfather but had reached their destination alone. His godfather had died along the path as old men often do, repeating their steps ever slower until the grave. They had made this pilgrimage to the Camargue coastline together many times and had fervently prayed to Sara e Kali there since Escher was a boy. But he had not prayed to the patron saint this year. He had simply reached the coast, bathed in the great *ser*, and put his godfather's black madonna amulet around his neck.

The amulet reminded Escher of the bygone songs his godfather used to sing in the shroud of moonlight and the campfire stories that set Escher's boyish imagination ablaze. His godfather would shuffle the leaden amulet between his callous fingers whenever he sensed trouble in camp or while he wooed mature enchantresses at famed carnivals. Escher remembered every place they had been when his godfather moaned that another Turkish eye bead had broken off the cord somewhere along their travels. Yet every imperfection endeared godfather to his amulet even more, because nothing makes us feel so whole and seen as a broken thing. But with his godfather gone now, the trinket offered Escher little solace amid his aimless drifting—as most things do when one is alone for the first time in so very long.

Earlier today, Escher had walked past deep and putrid pits on the outskirts of Pathyem—signs the village had seen a winter's plague. Scorched grass and gray ash lined the holes used to burn diseased corpses, stretching far into a barren field. An acrid smell festered in a spring breeze that held on to its winter bite. Escher had passed a fellow traveler who'd confirmed his intuition.

"I take it the worst is behind that poor town," the bumbling man had said in passing while strolling down the road outside of Pathyem, as if unsettled by the simple silence Escher preferred. "No sense dwelling on it though, always opportunities afoot somewhere else, innit?"

"For the ones still walking," Escher had replied gruffly. His eyes, the color of dark grapes, were sunken pits deep beneath his olive-skin brow.

Escher's curt reply didn't come from hatred toward his fellow man. Con artists are simply accustomed to looking out for themselves first. That's all. He'd help a person in need as much as the next man—if he thought he might finagle a reward out of it. If not, he enjoyed agitating folks—poking at the underbelly of their flaws and delighting in their discomfort. Yet he was always left unsated once they revealed the kind of selfishness that he hated knowing also existed in himself.

Nor did Escher mind the violence of a fight if unseen and a cinch—like now.

The passing traveler was portly with a well-groomed, twisted mustache. His grin curled as if his lips were divining for coin. "Oh heavens, not in paltry villages like this," the man had said with a dismissive chuckle. "Look to London. Even better, New York. They're not only walking, they're paying! And greed is nothing more than what poor folk call what their betters have rightly earned."

Escher's pace had remained unchanged. He had felt hostage to the man's futile conversation. Like a fugitive, he dared not look over his shoulder. But the pest had only turned 'round and followed to hound him longer.

"Tell me, my good man, have you heard of the spirit rappings?" the bothersome stranger had inquired. *Softly, softly, hear the rustle of the spirits airy wings,* the man had begun to sing along to a popularly catchy harpsichord tune in his head. *They are coming down to mingle, once again with earthly things.*

Spiritualism was indeed the talk of the era. True believers claimed they could communicate with the dead, a weighty proposition that tugged at the heartstrings of even the staunchest skeptics. Talk of hearing from the great beyond permeated the air like incense at a séance and filled tabloid literature like gore in a penny dreadful. But it paled in comparison to the insight that Escher could conjure.

With their rapping, and their tapping. Rap-tap-tap to wake our napping.

You see, Escher could deduce anybody's specific anxiety or fear, no matter how slight or disguised. Mind you, most of these intuitions came from little more than observing the human condition worldwide; but they were always correct, which was more than the Fruedians and fortune tellers could say.

Rap-tap-tap lost friends are near you; Rap-tap-tap they see and hear you.

Escher had known from the moment they encountered each other that this pesky man feared people would realize he wasn't as important as his grand gestures, fine-thread suit, and conversational soliloquy might portend. And Escher treated him as a lesser person because of it.

'Tis no fable—beings able—Rap-tap-tap upon a table, the man ended his haunting and off-key melody.

"Look. I'm going into whatever town this is," Escher had stopped and said with a spidery long finger pointed toward Pathyem. "Now I don't begrudge a man for making swindling greed his vice. We've all got our deflections. Best of luck. But mind you, we're not mates."

"Then we must be misunderstood, my friend!" the leech had started to bellow. "We spiritualist speakers seek the rapt attention of any heart yearning to call out beyond the veil. Those brave souls with passion, open-minds, sincerity, and the foresight to invest in the world that comes after death on this plane. Why, in my apothecary holdings I have enchanted candles for sale that can summon lost loved ones, shaman tonics for purchase that can induce dreams of old lovers, herbal aromatics on the cheap that enable any regular folk to communicate beyond into the spirit world and—"

But the man was soon startled by a flicker of blindness and a numbing head. The broken silence had set a hair trigger. Escher had closed the distance between them the same way he had finally silenced the man, with a clenched fist to the temple. That cold-cock punch was the last blow the man felt in the moment, numb to the kicks Escher hurled to his midsection as he fell unconscious. Vying for assets was a staple of Escher's mercurial life and survival. Sometimes out of necessity, other times out of opportunity. And there was no contest in this fight between peacock and snake.

The man's confusion peaked to panic once he awoke in a pit of ash and bone below ground—concussed, his nose bloodied, and his pockets disheveled.
The robbed man's coin was now destined for town in Escher's pocket.

***

EARLIER TODAY; WHERE WE MEET DARBY

Darby stepped outside her front door and swore with spite that could match the bitter cold. A murky, early-spring slush seeped into her old shoes and new stockings.

"*Kurwa masz,*" the woman cussed.

Darby was intimate with Pathyem's gray, cobblestone streets. She swayed past the residential palace, around the church where she was christened as a baby, and under the bell tower's astronomical clock. Pewter figurines of saints and serfs mechanically danced along their clockwork tracks as the bells rang seven times through a black morning.

She reached the entrance to a leaning building that had been on the city's less-fashionable edge for ages, since the townsfolk here were more meager. Her knife-nicked and burn-scarred hands nimbly sifted through a ragged hand-bag that never seemed to reach its fill. She clutched a set of ghoulish keys and unlocked the tavern door. Once inside, she opened the windows and let early daylight drip against the ancient, copper-tone clay walls.

Crooked shelves displayed baubles from when the building had been an antique shop—back before Darby's sister, Mona, had bought the place and turned it into a bar. Pocket watches along the far wall ticked together though they told different times. An armoire with rigid draw-ers hid heirlooms with no descendants and a fortune's worth of coins no longer in circulation. Darby dropped her threadbare bag beneath the mug rack and thought that she could do with an uneventful evening.

But undisturbed things are rarely left as they should be. And amid this city was a speck that would spawn a storm.

* * *

We romanticize places like people we miss, by ignoring their flaws.

Escher would long remember the evening he entered Pathyem, excluding the hapless man he'd robbed on his way into town. Sleight of hand magicians pawned a little brilliance for bewildered audiences in a pastel village center. Wraithlike light reflected off silty river water in a streetside canal. The air smelled of sour mushrooms, coriander earth, and transactional sin.

Souks in the medina's tight corridors swelled with dye and spice and blood. The sweltering stench of fish guts mixed with ripe citrus and fresh, porous bread that molded when each day died.

Escher found it serene. Foreshadowing is often modest—a most special hell.

He was thirsty. And the warming winds of spring drifted him toward the local tavern. Tobacco smoke clouded gaslights in the bar entry, casting a hazy light like the faint recollection of a distant memory.

Clientele rolled cigarettes to distract themselves from their more twisted vices. A frenetic bartendress carried trays of pint glasses with the grace and severity only a Pathyem woman could make look monotonous. A few drunks in the corner beckoned for refilled mugs and called out her name—Darby.

She returned to the scratched oak bar, where like an alchemist she turned copper coins into honey mead and gold pieces into old fashioneds. Escher sat at an open stool that wobbled against an uneven dirt and straw floor.

"Small glass Angel Rye, tall glass Porter," Escher ordered over the muffled sound of the buskers outside playing their minor-key melodies. He removed his gray, plaid flat cap and placed five copper coins from a nearly empty purse on the bar with a clink. The man he'd robbed outside of town had less money than Escher had hoped, but he hadn't expected much more either. Hucksters run on credit, con men on cash—they're just different grifts. The brawny woman behind the counter poured the clear spirit into a chipped shot glass and wiped foam off the beer mug with dispassionately little wasted motion.

"Any food here?" Escher asked.

"I keep tellin' everyone, not no more," Darby replied sharply. "Mona made the food, I pour the drinks. There's only one of us left now, so here are your bloody drinks."

The plague had depressed the tavern deeper than any burn pit outside of town. That much was clear to samaritans and misers alike who observed the isolated distance between people and the hushed tones of their heavy hearts.

Most people remember death as an event, but it doesn't feel like that to everyone. And it didn't feel that way to Escher either since he'd lost his godfather. To some, grief is a hole that seeths. Fire in the moment life fleets, numb as the memory fades. The dead are left frozen in the past while we must march on through the frost. Escher believed if death leaves behind questions that can't be answered, we best dare turn them into stories that can be carried through the cold.

"I knew a man from Glasgow," Escher began telling the disinterested bartendress. "In his younger years he'd been an adventurer of Arctic ice and sky. In his home-ridden years of old age he'd turned to making homemade wine, bottled pride that tasted like sweet vinegar. I think the heinous stuff had been strawberries once upon a time. His folks assured me when they offered me the bottles that he had poured his heart and soul into the hobby, but from the flavor he may as well have poured literal sweat and tears into them."

"We ain't busy. That don't mean I got time to lis'en. There's supposed to be a point to this story, innit?" Darby said with snappy impatience. Escher could tell she was underappreciated at best, marginalized at worst, and crossed at most ill-advised.

Escher took another long drink from the tar-pitch porter and inhaled the tavern air like it was sweet smoke from a tobacco barn.

"His kin didn't feel right drinking a dead man's wine, and they didn't want to hang on to something that wouldn't keep neither. Some folk are scared of good things, some folk are afraid of bad. But keeping it bottled don't keep it from being wretched," he said.

"Sentimental drunks be the worst," Darby said with percolating disdain as she carried another round of drinks to a corner table. When she returned to the bar, she was unamused at Escher's persistent prying.

"So then, why don't you tell me why you're scared of water instead?" Escher said, looking over the brim of his pint.

"What are you on about?" Darby asked. A blue vein in her neck pulsed in defensive tension.

"No washing pails in the kitchen from what I can see," Escher said, gesturing toward the back door. "But I bet there are a few empty ones out back waiting for whoever you got in for cleaning. Mind ye, they won't need it in here. Floor like this can't hold a puddle, and you been ignoring me by wiping this here bar with a rag that's as dry as shit in summer."

"You come here for water?" Darby asked pointedly.

"No," Escher said while running his fingers through thick and tousled black hair, fully enjoying the agitation he caused. Escher was keen. Fleet. A claw in the fog. A shadow swindler.

But not altogether great around people.

"Then what's it to you?" Darby asked as if she'd closed a trap.

"Call it gypsy intuition. Call it witty deduction. Call it my own little parlor trick, darlin'. I can tell ya' what I see—that you're scared of water. I can see what anybody's scared of and know I'm right. Knowing why is for psychics and shrinks, and that ain't me," Escher said.

Darby stopped, her attention shifting from barback work and toward Escher like water through a river lock. She only allowed this memory to resurface because she was unable to deny her curiosity toward Escher's mysterious perception.

"I seen a drunk old man drown in the river when I was a little gal. Since then I don't like water. And now I sink folk in a river of liquor," Darby said. "So that's me and my fear of water. And what would you be then?"

"Business," Escher replied, his cracked shot glass lifted and appreciatively tipped toward the bartendress, who finally allowed a wrinkly smirk to escape her defenses. "Nearly drowned once myself. Joined some train hoppin' boys and jumped into the river off a little cliff. My head clipped a rock when I landed a bit too close to shore. Been murky in the gourd ever since."

A few drops of the clear liquid landed on the bar as Escher drank the shot. He felt the burn and the cool and the numb before asking, "So, what happened here?"

"The plague—it caused a black lung," Darby said dryly, wiping the rye droplets off the bar. "Cough. Fever. Death."

"My sister Mona had a little one. She was fierce like a mama wolf. Her boy got to runnin' warm, so she took him to the bluestones," Darby explained.

"Bluestones? Here?" Escher asked.

"Just a circle of big fuckin' rocks," Darby replied. "Some dumb folk think 'em magic. Once the dying started, the old tales came back. People believin' again that touchin' the stones in the moonlight might heal. Mona's little one got worse. We knew what would happen, same as happened to Mama and the others 'round town."

The bartendress paused for a second, watching a few tavern guests stagger out of the door into the sort of cool, moonlit darkness that cradles drunkards to sleep.

"But I think for her the only thing worse than knowin' what was comin' was not doin' nothin' about it," she said, quieter than she had started.

"Bluestones," Escher echoed, nearing the bottom of his pint.

"She knew better. We all tried to stop her. But one night she bundled the boy up best she could and went walkin' to the stones. Middle of the freezin' win'er night. Not thinkin', just hopin'. She didn't come back next mornin'. Made it to the stones, but not back. They both died of cold just the same as dyin' of cough. Now I pour the drinks stronger, and nobody talks about the big fuckin' rocks anymore," Darby said.

Escher sat the empty pint on the bar, watching the mug rock and rumble against the uneven wood.

"Got any wine?" he asked.

"I think Mona was experimentin' with some," Darby said. "Warn ye, it might be heinous."

Escher put his last few coppers on the bar as another wobbling patron drifted toward the exit. Darby swept the coins off the bar into her rough hands and left. She returned from the kitchen with a green bottle while Escher planned a quiet place to sleep. The bartendress resumed her work, wiping tables with a dry cloth to dampen her thoughts. Escher pulled the cork with his teeth, sipped the harsh liquid, and slipped the re-corked bottle back into his coat. He straightened his flat cap, then tilted it downward.

"Mind me, stranger," Escher said to a drunkard under the lamplight outside the bar's entrance. "How far to the bluestones?"

THE ISLE

My numb feet staggered through moonlit fields of bouquet-ready daffodils that reflected midnight. I neared the circle of bluestone pillars that seemed insurmountable to the lingering, weighty fog. I slept there, among the spirits.

I dreamed. Visions of an island off the peninsular coast of Montezuma, where Pacific tides lap meekly against the pebbled shore. I bathed in the playa and rested on washed linens by the shore with Godfather. He explained to me that low tides recede for miles back into oceanic chaos, revealing a slippery rock path to Cemetery Island in the near distance. I watched as it rained on the isle of ancestors.

I remembered him saying there is a graveyard on the island that visitors can only reach in low tide. The faithful and the left behind must rise early and struggle through unforgiving sand and pasts. Guests of the dead then have precious few moments to visit salt-worn tombstones. They must flee the island before high tides arrive or risk becoming stranded with their grief—or worse, submerged along the path in the ocean's furious undertow.

Godfather told me the isle had been one of the many homes he'd made around nomadic campfires. His stories struck like flint to my heart's tinder. But where is that sense of home when the stories end?

It's easy to tell stories. It's difficult to make sense.

Godfather's image dissipates in my dream, and my calling out for him does nothing. Though the place is real, his presence here is sadly not. Like an isle that is always visible but only sometimes within reach.

***

THIS MORNING; WHERE WE MEET ZANDER

Escher startled. He was awakened by a stranger who didn't seem threatening—frail for middle age and wearing poorly fit sharecropper clothes—but that didn't make Escher much happier to be awake.

"Sorry to frighten ya' mister," the irritating man said. "I thought you was just admiring the bluestones."

Escher slid himself up and sat against a stone, admiring little more than the hangover he'd acquired from dead Mona's dodgy wine. He'd finished most of the nasty drink over the long walk to the bluestones—a lengthier trek than he'd anticipated. No wonder the mother and sick child hadn't made it all this way through the winter cold.

"Fascinating, aren't they?" the man continued. "You know, we still ain't even sure where they came from or even who brung 'em here."

"Wherever they were and whoever was here would be my guess," Escher said, his mouth dry.

"I hope I didn't disturb your work, communing with the spirits and all," the man said. "Places like this must have quite a shine for you spiritualists. Darby over at the tavern told me you come in last night. I figured I'd find you here. People says the place got real magic. Well, some folk anyway. You know about real magic mister?"

Hmmm, Escher groaned, lifting his lanky frame to stand against a stone wet with spring dew. Walking away seemed his best way out of this nuisance. Sharecroppers have already had most everything stolen from them, and wiry ones almost always surprise you in a fight. But Escher was quickly incentivized to continue the conversation.

"Well, Master Eli and me got your money either way, Doc. Can we go help Isla now?" the man asked.

Escher's drunken haze clarified to remember the braggadocious traveler leaving town that he'd beaten and dumped into a ditch. With the spiritualist rambler's grandiose sights set abroad and his candor toward the town's diseased winter, he must have left this job unattended. Escher was no believer in mediums, but he was most certainly a believer in cons—especially when light on money, like he was now.

"I'll take the first share now," Escher said authoritatively, seizing his con and his coin.

"The name's Zander," the sharecropper said, straightening his limp hat proudly lathered in a workmanlike coat of mud and plaster. "Follow me. The boss and his family'll be at home just past that field. You can stay at my place right across the crop if you like—softer than these stones."

* * *

MANY YEARS EARLIER; WHERE WE MEET ELI

Morning light briskly spread through every crack and crevice of the antique shop when the front door swung open. A young man hurriedly pushed through a modest doorway with boyish energy—shyly straightening his loose tie and too-small waistcoat once inside. He stiffened his back and proudly walked to an elderly woman behind a lone and gilded cash register.

"My name is Eli," the young man said with unearned authority. He removed a gray newsboy hat and brushed fair hair away from his eyes, which were open as wide as a fresh squire's. "I bear the surname of the manor atop the hill, and I've come with the intent of purchasing your quaint enterprise."

"I'll speak with your proprietor. Fetch him for me kindly," he said, removing leather gloves from unsubtly sweaty hands.

"You see anybody else here, boy?" the gray lady bucked.

Eli mimed a haughty resentment. "Don't think old age will permit you to forget good etiquette around your betters, crone," he said, stuffing his gloves in his hat and wafting nervousness as if it were a gas. "Now, I shall see your owner at once or leave him with a message of a time I may permit him to see me."

"Sonny, I run this here hole in the wall," the woman said. "This store began with my hoarder of a granddaddy. Mama took to selling it all as a way to clean out a junk inheritance. I've been opening that front door that give you trouble every morning for longer than you seen sunsets. And nobody been here to greet me in a purgatory minute. So there's no man here for you to posture for boy."

"Of course, pardon me for my forwardness," Eli said with diplomatic backpedaling. "A woman manager—to be commended in these progressive times." The woman smirked at the cold emptiness of the status quo.

"But surely you do not hold the deed," he again discriminated, though incidentally correct this time. "In whose name does this shop belong?"

"Like you folk would know," the woman said, waving her hand dismissively toward the hill where the elites and their brood like Eli lived in smug excess. "This lean-to has always been a place for the bits and pieces that a city remembers itself by. Never no owner here other'n dust and time itself."

"And the inventory?" Eli asked, incredulous toward his budding luck.

"Well, you can see we ain't short ah' nothin'," the woman replied, glancing over a shop so fit to burst that no two people could walk side-by-side. "Some things just find their way here: dropped by the doorstep, rediscovered in forgotten drawers, or pawned by them pauper kids I can't seem to say no to."

"So not only is your floorset a pig bin and your only shop window a rubbish marquee, but you acquire product from street urchins?" Eli said with an accusing crescendo.

"Everythin' in here got a story, that I bet you'll soon believe. And I wouldn't touch nothin' here unless it was falling on my head. And unless it blockin' the door on your way out, I recommend you don't neither," the shopkeep warned.

"Superstition and idle hands," Eli said. The sigh that followed mimicked his mother's palpable indignation toward commoners. "And what of the money, madam? I'd hope to at least see a ledger more useful than a sketchbook."

"I don't own nothin' in here, and people don't normally count things that ain't theirs ya' know. Them tax collectors got spooked off by tweakin' ruffians and stories about curses decades ago. I don't bother what money come in except to live off. I drop a copper piece for charity in the church box most days, a superstitious penny to the grim reaper street performer some days, and a pound for the food to get me here 'n back home. I don't want nothin' from this till to sully anythin' I rightly own."

What a discovery, Eli thought. *Surely a tribute of good fortune from God. Such an uncultured enterprise just within my reach – lacking merely proper ownership and sophisticated guidance. To think I came here ready to barter an inheritance; Now to find my stake will not only be for pennies what I expected necessary, but indeed charitable! Truly what fortune I carry in name alone.*

"Then madam, I offer you a proposal," Eli began in the Shakespearean grandeur of a community theater impresario.

"Your meager ways, truly to be admired even among the patron saints of modesty. Your work, although unrefined, is a testament to the hardiness of your everyday class. But have you not considered my dear a time for rest, or dreamed of the lavishness of a kept home with cotton comforts? Why not retire to the peace your years deserve and of the work you've done with the talent afforded you? Madam, I offer you just that."

"Why, with such an arrangement I could finance a maid-servant, a decor worthy of your earned rest, the warmth of luxuries befitting your home's four walls, and a humble stipend to support your noble ways. Is this offer nothing short of a dream? For your bauble shop madam, I can grant you my assurance it will be so for the rest of your days," Eli said with a matador's flourish.

The old woman closed her eyes. She remembered how as a child she thought her granddaddy had died because he got so bored. A tear formed in her left eye and fell for no one but herself, and she admitted to herself that this daily drudgery had become her idling in death's queue. She wouldn't let herself imagine a day where she didn't come in to work the shop, out of fear that if she stopped she'd end up dead and disregarded like her granddaddy.

"One day, you stop dreamin' of what might be and resign yourself to thinkin' that nothin' might be ever again; that's when you get old. Sometimes things ain't cohesive. Don't fool yourself into thinkin' they is. And don't always think you are neither," the woman said. "Old age is closin' shop on me and there ain't much better option than what you're offerin'. How about we mind the shop together? For what while I got left, that is. What exactly do you plan to do here?"

"Perhaps too complex for you to follow," Eli said. "But as added compensation for your compliance, I shall tell you of a future surely beyond your years or imagination. I shall personify a mercantile showman the likes of which Pathyem has never seen. The less educated here have never poured over the Romantics. Or even glimpsed the nuance of the Classics! A man with my talents? Why, I could sell these little black leaves to faux connoisseurs as aromatics from China—or these bags of rancid greens to naive mischief-makers as hashish from Tangier. Why, I will be able to spin a tale for every item in this shop until it's an irresistible lot."

"The poors..." Eli began, before bashfully bowing his head beneath the shopkeep's firm glare, "Of which you of course will have ascended through your hard labor and this good fortune...they always spend their pithy coins on frivolous nonsense like what surrounds us. Nothing but nostalgia-laden knick-knacks. Whereas I am a man of dispassionate business sense. Indeed, the populus will line around the shop from morning through gaslit evenings to empty their pockets until this store becomes my brimming coffer."

"Ah, I think I understand," the woman snickered like a dame to a shriveling member. "You'll be a circus barker."

"Of course not! Why, I'll be an antique Gatsby," Eli said. "I'll have you know that once emptied of everything, this shop will become the beachhead of my enterprise. Why, I can use this storefront as an emperor's throne room. Flush with commoner coin and notoriety, I'll conquer the business landscape of this whole damn street. I will be hailed by the district as a real self-starter—an example for the determined among the destitute and a shining light for the hands-on-clay builders of society. And it all starts here. Just here and me."

"And through what means will you achieve such adoration?" the woman asked.

"Through my father's money, of course!" Eli whined with a newborn's sense of perspective.

He beamed with pleasure and self-assurance, then extended his arm to assist the old woman around the corner of the register. "Very well, my employee. If you would be so kind as to show me around my new kingdom's stock and borders."

SADLY, SALT AND SMOKE

WHERE WE MEET CHLOE

Mother's screaming woke me up. I still skittishly tense when I remember that terrible sound. The angle of the moonlight against my window sill meant baby Chloe usually cried by now, hungry or in need of changing. But that night my mother desperately called for my father—her shriek a frightful exhale like air escaping a punctured lung.

I crept out of bed—gingerly, like the way my father would the morning after a hard day plowing the fields. I wrapped the woolen blanket my grandmother had knit for baby Chloe around my boyish, bony shoulders.

My parents stood over a cradle that rattled from a terrible cough. I saw through the cradle rails that baby Chloe's marble gray eyes were open but dull and unable to focus on mother's tear-streamed face. Drool oozed and foamed down my sister's plump cheeks, which were flush pink. Her puny fists shook weakly as she struggled to breathe and she kicked in convulsion when she had yet to take her first steps.

My parents checked baby Chloe's breathing, her pulse, her fever, and held each other tight.

My father rarely yelled at me.

"ZANDER! Go fetch a coupla' leeches boy!"

Soooooie! I hopped right out the door! I did and I was knee high in the ditch kicking up mud 'fore I remembered I's still wearing them socks I got for Christmas just a month before.

Course, then I got cold.

I'd know I had a leech bite when I felt a little prick and then it'd start to tickle. I'd wait just a second until I'd get to feeling funny, then hop on out the ditch and pull them leeches off my skinny legs like ticks. "Just like fishing," my father had told me. The doctor had told us that leeches was good for all sorts of ailments.

Usually I'd just wade around on a summer day for a while to get out of doing field work. But never straight out of bed! And I couldn't wait for a nibble that night. I had to make sure baby Chloe was okay. That's what big brothers do.

"God dammit boy!" Father yelled when I came back inside with no leeches. I pretended that I was still sleepy and booger-eyed to hide that I was crying. I was scared. I didn't turn 9 until that next summer.

I watched Father draw a penknife from ragged overalls that hung in the corner while Mother nervously rocked baby Chloe and held down her pale, chubby arm. My stomach turned all squirmy when I saw Father cut baby Chloe's pillowy skin. She cried and convulsed while Father made the cuts that he hoped would save her life. Dark crimson blood flowed from her porcelain limb and dripped into the nighttime darkness. The stain never got out of them floors. And I ain't never been good with handling the sight of blood since.

"We'll let the bad blood out just as good as the doc would, baby," Father told Mother. "Hold her tight. We're all gonna' be alright."

Mother squeezed baby Chloe's arm. I gave her Grandmother's coarse blanket to wipe the blood away. My eyes were too wide to cry.

Baby Chloe stopped shaking. I didn't understand why Mother was kissing her so hard—like she was making baby Chloe breathe her air.

"Go back to bed, Zander," my Father told me. "You n' me got a long day in the fields when sunup. And I want you ready for workin', ya' hear?"

"Your sister gonna' be alright," he added with a shakily unsteady voice, shielding Mother and quiet baby Chloe in his shadow. This was the first of many nights marred by my sister's ghastly seizures.

I didn't get hardly a lick of shuteye that night. I rolled around in that bed like I was tryin' to sleep through a squall. It felt like my head was sinking to the very bottom of some dirty pond. I didn't want my sister to go to heaven; not yet I mean. That ain't a bad thing to think—is it? But thinkin' it over n' over, it just *kept makin' everything in me all worked up and worse. Like I was tryin' to pull a fishin' line through a mess a' limbs.*

I figured that night done snapped whatever little pole of a spirit I had in me.

Of all the futures that never happened, hers is still the one I miss the most.

* * *

Zander guided Escher to an estate between freshly plowed farmland and a towering cliff overlooking Pathyem. A lighthouse-style turret accentuated a precariously placed Victorian mansion upon the hill. The tightly tongued porch slats creaked under foot but gave little weight. Escher picked a splinter of bark off the wooden frame as Zander rapped the front door.

A gray and hardened man opened the door, an elegantly mustached figure made solemn by propriety and pretension.

"Zander," the man said like a belittling headmaster, "here to no doubt raise the repute of my humble home."

Escher recognized the boot-heel stench, the common fear of appearing weak in front of others. He had met many men, and a minority of caustic women, chained to this fear. They most often replied as if life, and particularly vagabonds like Escher, were beneath them. Escher sensed the man considered Zander in this disreputable class as well. This man was the antithesis of what Godfather believed to be a good person, and he reminded Escher of the darker parts of himself. A stray, black cat jumped onto the porch near the door. The bitter man kicked it back to the ground.

"Eli," Zander said with the faintness of a man apologizing for his existence. "I found your doc Escher in town like ya' pay me for. I knew the family'd be in an awful hurry."

"Do I look like I need a doctor, boy?" Eli said, dismissing Zander's manhood and posturing for a stranger. "I take it this shadow with you is the charlatan that's supposed to save us all," he added, his jaded eyes fixed on Escher.

Eli was a joker. Unfunny, he was a jester. A narcissist exuding a noxious vapor of self interest that mist on those around him. Like a royal unworthy of their salt.

Beverly was made of that salt.

She harnessed the frailty and ferocity of a mother. She maneuvered in her husband's shadow, the cavernous darkness beneath Eli's roaring waterfall of vanity. Her hair was short and tightly bound, bobbed for function and worn gracefully. Her face was wrinkled like proof of patience. The weathered wife dutifully welcomed the men inside, where her hearth maintained a small fire that boiled inviting loose-leaf tea.

Escher's skilled perception wasn't necessary for determining the fear behind Beverly's downcast eyes, shallow blue pools marred by chronic tears. Her smile was a sham, covering the frantic optimism of a mother living with a terrorizing anxiety—waiting on another doctor unlikely to save her child. She remained silent while Eli dominated a conversation he felt he'd paid for. Beverly didn't listen, just quietly measured Escher as if unsure how to balance her scales teetering between suspicion and hope.

She will be an easy con, Escher thought. He rarely pitied himself because he believed it would induce vulnerability. Although he pitied Beverly a little, his desire to profit from her distress far exceeded his empathy.

"Woman, now why the hell are you prepping house for this monkey?" Eli said as his tirade marched on. "You know people like him are nothing more than irredeemable professional felons. And I'll be damned to see him thieving anything I've earned out of hard and honest work."

People like Eli blame outsiders for all social ills, an ever-shrinking core of puritans targeting people on ever-receding fringes. *This is how people end up shot.*

"I want to make myself perfectly clear," Eli declared. "I do not believe in you, *Doctor* Escher, or any of you spiritualist swindlers. Your ghosts and your psychics are nothing but voodoo tricks for feeble-minded fools. I've made up my mind about that girl, and she's set for the lunatic hospital upstate. I only summoned you here at my fragile wife's behest. Money spent on a spook like you isn't nearly as much of a consideration to me as the impediment two hysterics under the same roof would bring to my reputable name."

For a Romani to survive, it isn't enough to just be clever. If that were the case then Escher would have been born with the key to a relatively easy life among nomads. He'd acquired a half dozen languages by a half dozen years old. Not just that, but he had also cultivated his skills of being cunning and sly since he was little—tending them with the watchful attention of a destitute farmer over early spring crops. But no. For a Romani like Escher to live, silence was required more often than skill. Godfather had reminded Escher since he was young that it was not in his best interests to introduce their habits to the *gadjo* around him. He scratched his chest to subtly make sure his black madonna amulet hadn't come untucked from beneath his shirt.

"Then shall we proceed with the formality of seeing the patient?" Escher replied with his best guile, unbothered by Eli's deprecating attitude. It would only hasten Escher's con.

"The child is in a coma," Eli said flatly. "Your services will be noted and quickly rendered. I'm off to see a stable hand about a thoroughbred and will be home by sundown. I'll expect your answer and then your absence." His outstretched arm directed Escher to the end of a shotgun hallway before he strode away toward a chauffeur carriage awaiting him.

"Isla started seizing in the winter, just after last Christmas," Beverly said, her eyes cast down to the beetle rot floorboards. "I was...we thought it was the plague. But my girl is strong, Doctor Escher. She's cold and still in the bed more days than not now, but she's still in there. It's what come out of her that scares me like no mother wanna' admit."

"Scares?" Escher inquired, reaching for a loose doorknob to the girl's bedroom where Beverly had stopped.

"Escher," Zander said hesitantly, his rough hand turning Escher's shoulder to face him.

"We lost the town doc last winter to the cough, but Isla...well...what Isla do even the doc couldn't have helped,"

Zander said in a hushed tone, stagnant amid astonishment and fear.

"My Isla's in there, but sometimes her voice ain't," Beverly began to explain.

"The voices started 'fore the spring crops went in the ground. I sat by her bed a lot then, thought they might be part of her fever dreams and seizing fits. But her eyes, sometimes her eyes change color when it ain't her voice. Sometimes she sound like a gristle old man worse than Eli. Lord forgive me. Sometimes she sound like a little girl again. Sometimes she sound like a devil witch."

"One time, Eli heard her speaking some blasted foreign tongue don't nobody understand, and he raised hell tellin' her to wake up or shut up. Word got around town like it always do, and the newspaper man come down here to string us up by ink. Said it was all fake. But Isla spoke in some voice that read aloud a letter in the reporter's vest pocket – word for word – without him even sayin' it in there. He about trip himself out the door in disbelief. Eli paid him to not write nothin'."

"Eli wanna pretend she do it for attention, says she almost believable enough for a roadshow like them Fox sisters. Says not even Houdini could say Isla don't do what she do. Then says she's too hysteric n' lazy to make money off her. But he's serious about sendin' her to the asylum way out where nobody see. With them animals. That's why I sent for your kind Escher. Spiritualists, that is – I don't mean no offense. My Isla is sick, and mamas don't know how to pretend they kids ain't hurting."

Escher turned back to the bedroom door, breaking contact with Beverly's hollowed eyes. He entered the homey bedroom as if he was stepping into the cage of a sleeping lioness.

SICKNESS WAKES

WHERE WE MEET THE KEROAX

Motes of ash from the burn pits on the outskirts of town drifted on the wind, particles of deceased people floated through an open window into Isla's slacked-open mouth. The monstrous Keroax had possessed many a neurotic spirit since the dawn of cremation rituals, but never once an empath like the sickly girl confined to a yellow-wallpapered bedroom in Eli's house upon the hill.

This will make a splendid consciousness from which to conquer all.

A necromantic, amber glow hooked around the small of Isla's back. It pinned her down as if to an ocean floor, and from the darkness of a coma she floated under the glare of the telepathic mephit's gray stare.

Isla. Dame of the damned. Do you believe birds chirp when the foxes catch them? Or only before they realize they've been snared?

*In this way you shall understand the Keroax: Whatever demons
you believe there to be, they exist within the ether that is we.*

* * *

Isla was no child. The sleeping young woman's sickly figure
belied her imposing presence. Though still and serene
against clean cotton sheets, she emanated power and radi-
ated the horror of terminal illness. Standing by her bedside,
Escher saw bruises and raised scars on her left arm like debris along a porcelain-banked river. Blood stained her wrist
as if pain could leave patina.

That's when the thrashing started. The convulsions of a
seizure that contorted her body into a frayed ribbon of flesh
and stretched sinew.

Beverly wasted neither time nor motion. She inserted
the gnawed handle of a wooden ladle between her daughter's grinding teeth and dabbed foamy saliva from the edges
of her lips with a soiled, handmade cloth. She did all of this
with just one hand, the other grasping Isla's hand with a
steadiness that could defy an ocean's pull toward the abyss.
The bed smelled of waste.

"How often does this happen?" Escher asked in the bari-
tone of an aloof physician to maintain a convincing con.

"Every day," Beverly said. "More 'n once more days 'n not.
Sometimes she stays quiet afterward. But silence ain't peace
for a mother. I'll be here fearin' the worst until Eli calls me
to make supper. Then I jus' worry while busy."

Isla's violent shakes rattled the bed like rough love. Beverly wet the cloth for Isla's fevered brow.

"Sometimes she wake, but I don't let her see no tears those days," Beverly said.

Isla's thunderous shakes began to subside. Her petite frame would sporadically twitch like the explosion of a blunderbuss into a lake that would absorb the shot and settle into stillness once more.

"But I listen every time Doctor Escher, even in the middle of the night, in case I hear a voice that ain't welcome here. And it be gettin' worse. Much worse," Beverly said, nervously waiting for her child to wake.

What woke wasn't Isla for long.

A rigor mortis stiffness overtook Isla's stretched frame along with a sharp gasp. The sweet voice that followed dripped slowly like sap from a lightning-struck tree.

"I must be the only girl in Pathyem whose mother brings strange men straight to her bedroom," Isla said with a wry smile toward Beverly, grateful for her tender care.

Beverly smiled back, but Escher could still sense tension in her shallow breaths. The con-man doctor turned back to Isla, surveying her eyes and their shade of green like skies ready to burst with hail.

"Zander," Isla said, breaking eye contact with the Romani to greet the sharecropper. "Lovely to see you. Pity it had to disrupt such a delightful dream."

Escher raised an eyebrow from its usual, cynical furrow. Isla's pleasant demeanor and witty conversation seemed rather chipper considering she'd recently dismounted a seizure, no matter how often she suffered the grand-mal malady. He began to wonder if it was indeed all just an act.

Had this trickster vixen and her convincing mother planned to con the real spiritualist doctor that Escher had ruthlessly tossed into a pit? *Eh, he's probably fine*, Escher dismissed the distracting thought.

"Sorry to wake you ma'am," Zander replied courteously. "What was your pretty lil' head dreamin' 'bout?"

"I dreamed that I was in heaven. Not the place with a bunch a' hymns and Bibles and stiffs—the place where everybody's happy. I saw my little brother. He was fishing with Papa, who said I keep growing like a weed—just like he always does," Isla said. "Then I woke up and saw you here, Mis'er Escher. That sure is a pretty pendant 'round your neck."

"Hello Isla," Escher said, pulling a chair to her bedside. He disguised his surprise that she knew his name and had somehow noticed the hidden amulet. People who noticed his black madonna usually thought it some blasphemous patron of *muerte* or were confused by its unusual material—a rare and unmeltable carbide on a thread-thin gold chain. *How could she see right through me?*

"I was unaware that we'd met," Escher responded, lifting her wrist under the pretense of checking her pulse.

"We haven't, until now at least," Isla said, sitting up in bed despite Beverly's silent protest and gentle hand on her shoulder.

Escher reached for a medicine bottle on the nightstand. He opened a tincture of fermented pomegranate seeds and rubbed some of the oily red smear on his gums. He nodded, a satisfactory quality check of the medicine masking his penchant for morphine.

"But up there," Isla continued, nodding upward, "you kinda get to know everybody."

"Is that so?" Escher said, irked that his patronizing tone sounded like Eli. "Well, consider me thrilled to know there's a place for me in the clouds."

Isla giggled, a schoolgirl's laugh hiding a secret everyone knows but you. "You're not the happy type, Mis'er Escher. People who walk as many miles as you rarely are once they lose count. And if you'd listened, you'd know I said that when you're up there you get to know everybody. I didn't say that everybody was up there."

"You see, I got all these spirits in my head. But trying to hear their voices is like watching raindrops on a window—you can track 'em, but they don't last long. So I try to keep the pretty ones intact and let the bad voices drain away."

"But they're coming, Mis'er Escher. Don't matter if you're in Pathyem or been to Zanzibar. Papa warned me, they're coming for us all," Isla said.

"Who's comin'?" Zander asked.

"What else did Papa say?" Beverly added, doing her best to keep a tear from falling.

CRACK! Isla's head snapped back against the headboard and her jade eyes turned milky, cataract white. She began to choke and convulse as Beverly sprang to attention.

Escher could see the exit of a quick and cleanly executed con. It was obvious that the girl…woman…had lost her grip on sanity. Equally apparent was that no doctor between here and London itself could heal her hysterics. And no doubt Eli would scoff at the price of trying to cure her when she'd be out of sight and mind for far less at the asylum. *Eli's word will be law and his coin will be mine.*

Isla groaned from decrepit pain and slumped over. A shrill German accent took over her tongue and blitzed foreign obscenities that amused Escher until the curses flew toward him.

"Christ," Zander said. "That sounds like ole' Meena Pearl. That ole' crone chewed me out but good when I's a boy for sneakin' some soured apples off her land. But she died of cough!"

Beverly's head sank into the dark uncertainty that follows lost causes.

"Yes, she did," Beverly confirmed. "Just as certain as them dirty rumors 'round town that Isla shake and speak gibberish. But the voices are real, Doctor Escher. And I need you to get in that girl's head and get my Isla back."

Isla sprang to the front of the bed with the force of a raging child. A small lump appeared in her throat as a young boy's voice shrieked, "They're coming! They're coming quick!" Beverly and Zander stumbled back against the bedroom wall, shocked by the voice that screamed like the first second after a nightmare. Escher stood up quickly. His confused, flailing arm knocked his chair backward.

A darkness began festering in the bedroom. A fungal smell of rot and bulbous trails of mold began spreading across the bed and onto Isla herself. Her diseased body writhed to levitate above the bed. Zander had long since stopped looking. Beverly stood in terror-struck stillness as her daughter's illness morphed into something impossible—something she had never seen and even worried mothers couldn't imagine. The insidious eventuality that had emptied Isla and turned her into a petrified vessel in front of their eyes announced itself.

"*I AM THE KEROAX!*"

Escher was enthralled. *Would you look at that. Something almost as bewitching as me.*

"Now you see, the thing about nomads is..." Escher began, wresting control from the deranged spirit like a feral horse, "we see frightening things in unfamiliar places all the time. And we say, 'Eh, what the hell...must come with the territory.' We get on with it. But it's 'cause we got old, old stories to ground us. I reckon' Isla's got her share too. Stories about what lives in the night and the sea and the..."

"Ash..." he said, crestfallen. Isla was being transformed, her smooth-skinned features now mimicked by a smoldering glow. Her cheeks became a swirl of embers and her tongue a blackened weapon. It spoke—a sound like the cavernous echoes of many voices. Escher could have sworn he heard Godfather's voice somewhere in the disjointed harmony.

"The Keroax have risen from the souls of your burned. We are the phoenix of your lost consciousness. The air from your plagued lungs ignited us. Soon we heard our kin rotting in the ground and sought to revive them. We grow and become emboldened by your fire pits of disease. We are the condensation of cremation. We seek a human vessel strong enough for us to kindle everything. The bodies below shall have a consciousness again and the spirits within us will possess all," it declared.

"And you've noticed the third option around here, the live ones?" Escher said, waving for Beverly and Zander to scatter out of the bedroom door now covered in black mold.

"What happens to the rest of us?" Escher demanded.

"What do you think death feels like?" the Keroax answered with a question.

Escher stood his ground in the silent, pestilent-ridden bedroom with Isla. The vines of infection were now retreating back into the ashen figure. He thought about his Godfather's passing and the slashing pain he'd felt in his gut when he knew Godfather was gone.

"It feels...like being ripped in half," Escher said.

"Then you already have your answer," the Keroax replied as it cast Isla back onto the bed like a parasite ditching a drained host. Her body healed over, smooth and amorous skin covering over what had just been an array of rot. But the putrid smell remained. The monster and the blight it cast upon the bedroom dissipated into smoke and spores that vapidly vanished. Escher braced against the wall amid the silence of a passed storm. Isla's disheveled red hair wisped over the bedside as she slept in childlike peace. Springtime sunlight lit the yellow room softly as he stepped out and closed the bedroom door behind him. A noxious, sulfuric smell wafted into the hallway. Beverly and Zander huddled close and worried in whispers.

"Good as dead and done for," Escher said, lips pursed like the tightly shut bedroom door. His hands rifled through his coat pockets for a small metal case and a pack of matches. He opened the tin and ran the tip of a clove cigarette over his lips before he lit more smoke and hung the coat on a slightly crooked rack.

"I think we should ask the vicar for help," Zander said assertively, speaking on behalf of a rattled and whimpering Beverly.

"Fine," Escher answered with a deep exhale of tobacco smoke. He knew he would have to wait a few hours for Eli's payment anyway. "Church will be as futile as anything else."

THE HAUNTED AND HOLY

MANY YEARS EARLIER;
WHERE WE MEET THE VICAR

A drunk man staggered through the narrow door of the bauble shop late one evening, disgraced as the drink allows and in need of a distraction. He accidentally knocked over a few items near the door on his way in. Despite his disfigured hand, he tried to steady the trinkets back in their place – the sort of tiny sin only saints and drunkards stop to fix.

Young Eli sprang toward the door, ready to befall another customer like a new ax in the hands of an experienced executioner. But the old shop assistant patted him on the forearm to slow his enthusiasm for a sale. "Now I know ya' think every moment is a coin gained or lost. But don't pay Phiri no mind," the old woman said. "He won't hurt nothin', and he been through enough already to go spendin' what little money he got just for your till, Eli."

"Blast it woman. For here, any man or woman from this downtrodden land can find something to take their cares away," Eli replied.

"Don't pretend you know what it's like for folk down here, under the shadow and the thumb of you rich folk from up the hill," the old woman began in a hushed tone while the drunk man pretended—poorly—to stoically browse the shop.

"Phiri—he's lost. Not in the physical sense—slavers done plucked him from beneath the baobab tree in the middle of his village long ago. And the church took him after he was maimed and of no use to the slavers. No—Phiri, he's lost in that spiritual sense—like a sheep having strayed from the flock. Except for him it be much worse, because he's a backslidin' preacher. People pity a lost soul; but a shepherd failin' his congregation? Why, it must feel like a weight heavier than sin."

"Phiri had a beautiful and beloved wife, Estrellita Bell was her name. And she was a walkin' daybreak of a lady, let me tell you. But she done collapsed by their bedside one stormy summer evening. Only one doctor in the whole wetlands would take a look at her on account of her color. And after taking twice the money he'd charge a white woman, the doctor told Phiri there was nothin' he could do nohow. The doctor said her blood had gone thick and made sticky shards of death all up in her heart and lungs. She died before the dawn. Some folk say it was weeks before Phiri clean the sheets of the blood she'd coughed up that night."

"The congregation had mourned—flowers and hotplates delivered to the preacher's front door every day for a solid month. All of them must have smelled like nothin' and tasted like nothin' to him. The petals wilted and fell on the floor beside bits of chicken and rice that went rancid. I still remember the smell when I done checked on him once. They say it wasn't long before a bottle found its way beside his Bible. Then several empty ones. The congregation forgave him for sermons that sputtered, but turned on him when his words became slurred. As soon as sympathy in time of need was no longer fashionable, the deacons told him he'd fallen to the devil and whispered worse once they closed the church doors behind him," the old woman concluded.

"Nevermind such trivial things," Eli said, his arms motioning out and creating a foreground to the cluttered store behind him.

Eli grabbed the nearest items that caught his attention as he dragged Phiri around the shop like an ox calf. "So, what'll it be for you? Fancy sights around the world via these postcards? Or perhaps pornography from unsung silver screen starlets? Or maybe a decent man's clothes from the finest Birmingham textiles?"

Eli could press on through Phiri's boozy fog and turn his shopping distraction into an inevitable purchase.

"Well, I suppose some'ting to read might be nice," Phiri said.

"And a reader you say?" Eli said incredulously, "I suppose we'll be looking more along the side of picture books than the classics now won't we." He pulled the preacher toward a dusty and half-broken bookshelf. After a perusing moment, he made a show to gently remove the first Bible he saw—a wrinkled leather tome that he pretended to cradle with the tenderness of a runt puppy.

"To take nothing from the masters of the arts; but what are they when compared to the words of our creator? Am I right?" Eli said rhetorically.

"Not sure," Phiri said with a cracking slur that leaked honesty as booze so often does. "I used to listen for de Lord for days on end. Use to t'ink every time it rain it must be raining de whole world over just like de Noah flood. Years t'inking de Lord might speak to me some night. I t'ink I just find comfort in de rhythm of religious t'ings. I hate it. I be feelin' righteous with all them rituals and routines. It can make you feel better than folk, but it's all just puttin' on airs to beat Moses. It be no different den money dat way. But dat whole life be damn fragile, when Jesus and luck be showing up and disappearing together joined at de hip. Makes me t'ink maybe der just ain't no voice to hear."

"Now you listen to me like the good book says. Of course the good Lord got a voice in the winds!" Eli said. "Now why else would the breeze have brought you here today? I tell you, this here Bible belonged to my own dear, devoted mother."

"Yep," Eli continued his ruse. "Read it to me on her knee every night and beat my backside with it more than once when I was a boy, she did. And I tell you this, hand over my heart and the other on the cover — every time that woman turned to a verse it either came true to life or was exactly the advice one needed to do the good Lord's work."

Phiri was not so drunk as to believe lies like this. But at the sight of a Bible—the scripture he'd ignored for so long now—he hunched lower and the booze welled to tears in his eyes. "I do miss hearing de Word from a good woman's lips."

Eli slid the Bible between Phiri's hands, then backed away from the reeking drunk. "The Word never fails."

Phiri pressed the book to his chest and sighed with great relief. "Praise da Fader, de Son, and de Holy Spirit."

"Praise indeed," Eli agreed. "And shall we say, 30 crown kuna and a handful of zwolts?" He took the cash and coin from the drunk preacher's shaking hand and watched the door shut. Young Eli opened the gilded register and deposited his first sale.

He closed the shop early that night and celebrated the achievement by lighting and choking on a few puffs of his first cigar.

* * *

Zander led Escher down one of Pathyem's uneven brick roads, avoiding the scattered missing bricks without a single glance down. Yellow dandelions sprang up from cracks in the street and cottonwood floated in the air across a horizon of countryside green. After a few miles, the silent pair walked around the bend of a low stone fence just tall enough to pen white, wooly sheep. Churchgoers quietly shuffled past them, their foreheads marked with ash. To Escher's perception, the repentance ritual branded people with their sins more than it absolved them. Adulterer. Idolator. Glotton. Saddled by guilt, not unyoked from their burdens like the pulpit had promised.

"It's not much," Zander finally broke the silence, "but it's been good to me and most folk 'round town."

The small and carefully tended chapel looked like it was built from barely more than white slats held together by hardened clay and a few devouts. The afternoon sun cast a golden light around the grounds, which were kept in meticulous, workmanlike beauty.

The church door creaked and the plainly decorated interior was mostly empty. Zander bowed his head as he walked in and waved his hand over his chest in repentant routine. Escher followed behind him and did nothing. An antiquated wooden confession box against the wall loomed like a torture rack. An elderly, faithful woman exited one side of the leaning box, whispering penance for quiet regrets.

"Preacher Phiri he…well he kinda do things his own way. But he's a good man. He's in there for everybody," Zander said. "You oughta see the ruckus he can cause on a Sunday mornin'. He can say all of Exodus from memory and tell Br'er Rabbit tales about divine intervention. Those are my favorites. It'd shock a lesser man to see how many white converts flock to a colored clergyman's invitation to join in the sinner's prayer."

"I'm not the religious kind," Escher answered. "But if believing helps you sleep at night and work good in the morning, then you go on ahead. Tell the man what you saw, then I'll see what he's got to say."

Zander went into the confession box with the hopeful desperation of a sailor boarding a life raft.

* * *

Escher paced. He felt that he didn't belong here, just as he had the first time he'd entered a church. And every one after. The walls were painted a drab, sickly sage. Simple pine pews in two neat rows left a lone aisle down the middle—a path that had been walked by more pallbearers than brides recently. The stained-glass window above the lonely podium looked as brittle as the dried husk of a deserted wasp nest.

Escher was alone. Or maybe conflicted. Same thing really. *I could leave with the coin Zander gave me at the bluestones while he spills his guts in that fool's box. There's enough here for a horse out of this cursed, beat town. There's enough left over for a few night's keep and company in bed. How long has it been since I've tasted a hot meal? I'll be clean and gone, and nobody will follow me.*

He wanted to believe that he hadn't left yet because he could still return to Eli and get the rest of his coin, the type of sum that could tide him across an ocean. But what sort of adventure would he be able to find abroad that could outmatch the monster he'd just seen?

What was it Godfather always used to say? "Anything in front of ya' that ain't family or clan is a con." When I was young, it was so simplistic that it sounded like the mantra of a master. He taught me to read on a storybook about a shepherd who ventured into the desert in search of a fortune. And the stories he told around the campfire to me and the other scamps recounted so many wondrous places and mysterious people. Before we knew it the skinned hedgehogs he'd rolled in clay were baked and ready to mix with root vegetable and fermented cabbage stew. And I always felt safe with him.

As an adolescent, I thought the old man's mantra was just an excuse to avoid brawn-and-sweat work. Maybe it was just the kind of line we all come up with to keep us on the road. The way that man pulled stunts the world over. Remember that time he worked a derby in bluegrass land, then stole the track's prized thoroughbred and sold it to a sultan? He sold everything from shoddy hookah to novices in the Petit Soco to furs of Wroclaw bears for palace guards in Stockholm. "The key in life is to find work that you're good at and can withstand other people saying you should really be doing something else," he once told me. From then on I was a con man too.

For my first con he posed as a conductor on the Moscow-Vladivostok line and I pilfered things while pretending to be a luggage boy. We left the Russian cold and rode until the ice melted in Harbin. That was when I first realized I had the damndest perception. Godfather called them "saikik" powers and helped me hone my skill. I soon realized my ability to perceive what people were scared of meant I could be fairly sure of escape from any con, even if I did feel a bit guilty about using their fears against them. After a while I just kinda shut myself off from feeling that guilt. That made me think of bigger, more elaborate cons than the little grifts Godfather taught me. I was afraid I'd let him down. He didn't need my abilities to know that. Though he was a difficult man to impress, I think he only wanted me to enjoy the world and its people like he did—for our differences to have us both aligned in the joy of living in a wondrous world.

Godfather showed disinterest toward anything that wasn't grand, which is why there was no one else to mourn him at the end except me. And even then I know he mostly kept me around so he had somebody to show off to. I never told him what I knew, that he was afraid of living a boring life. He thought lives like the ones people here in Pathyem lead are like tasteless water, but they're drawn from wells that are deeper than a nomad like me could ever have the patience to dig. Once you've seen ferocious power like that Keroax, curiosity becomes more sentimental than nostalgia.

Maybe one day I'll be able to tolerate the uninteresting, but today is for the grand.

* * *

Escher felt a tap on his shoulder.

"Well, I figured he'd think me crazier than it seems he did," Zander said. "He in there waitin' for ya'. He says I best stay out here n' pray for us all."

The door to the confession box felt lighter than Escher had expected. He sat on a somber little bench and closed the flimsy box shut. *It really gonna be four walls, somethin' creepy, and me all day?* It was dark inside, save for the vomitous green curtain the vicar pulled open. Escher spoke through shadowy, wire-woven mesh holes. "Bless me Father, here I am."

The vicar's deep voice rolled low and thunderous as a Saharan lion. "Everyone in your chair face some sort of monstah. According to Mistah Zander, seems a real monstah in your case," he said.

Escher grinned and scoffed. "Zander thought you'd say he's crazy," he said.

"My world, every'ting crazy," Phiri answered. "But why should I be surprised, huh? You folk t'ink nothing real less it in front of you. Sometimes not even den. My brothers and sisters know monstahs walked this earth long before we do."

Escher watched the priest gesture in holy reverence, his right hand missing a thumb and a forefinger. Escher grimaced at the mental image of the vicar's excruciating fear—a sugarcane press flowing red amid the sound of snapping bones and screaming agony. He could barely make out that the priest wore no white collar beneath his tight black hair and craggy face.

"You? In this box?" Escher said. "Second strangest thing I've seen today – smack between that monster and me sittin' here with ya'."

"My brothers and sisters and me—we not here by choice. But I got faith my own way. De old priest here, he died of all dat mess and tragedy dat happen almost every winter here. I used to tend da grounds, now I tend de flock," the vicar said. "Sometimes de good Lord gives us second chances, least on some t'ings."

"And how's the flock taking that?" Escher asked with realistic skepticism.

"Men like dat Eli you meet, he roars and writes letters to more men like him. Says it hurts de whole town worse den plague if de church don't have a priest proper and white. So far nobody answer his letters—nobody want to come here when there's work with de dying. But most people come to church anyway because dey got nowhere else to go. And dat what church here for anyway," Phiri said.

"Zander said we should come to you for help. What kinda help did you give him? He hasn't even left a pew yet," Escher said.

"Person can do a lot from a pew," the vicar replied. "If dey heart right."

"And what'll it do for Isla? What'll it do to the monstah bigger 'n you and me?" Escher demanded.

"Give us de hope to fight and da peace to lose," Phiri said. "We can't know what monstahs are out there, or what happens to us when dey come. But da faith can be there if we want, and tomorrow promise not'ing else."

Escher paused. Considered. Then refused.

"Belief in God is a box," Escher replied. "Everything that terrifies us, everything we don't know, everything you refuse to look at. Everyone you can't stand to talk to and every change that scares you shitless, all stowed away in the box."

"Then you hold it up. You adorn the box. You pride yourself on the conceited decorations in place of the wonders you locked away. You warn that embracing others who don't bow before the box will unleash unspeakable evils hidden inside the box—the monsters you pretend come from somewhere other than the swamps of your own imagination. And you die for that box—unwilling to unpack it for fear it might lighten others' load."

"Here is my confession, priest," Escher answered. "I will not be ashamed of my hope."

"Then together we hope our own ways are enough to stop de monstahs," Phiri replied. "You know where to find Mistah Zander. And you know where to find me. In the name of da Fader, de Son, and de black madonna." Escher smirked and tugged at the amulet that had slipped out from beneath his shirt.

"We've all got our superstitions," Escher confessed.

Escher closed the chapel door behind him and walked toward a violet sunset. Zander stayed faithful and behind.

NO MORE TIRED HORSES

A FEW MONTHS EARLIER

"You're being unreasonable," Isla argued.

"I know it isn't fair!" Beverly replied with a parent's exasperation. "But you can't leave this house again without me."

"Will you calm down? It was just a dance! It's not like I have some secret beau. It's not like I'm with child. It was just a Saint Valentine's dance to get us all through this dreadful, cooped-up winter," Isla explained. "That's all. What's wrong with that?"

"What's wrong is we don't know when these seizing fits hit like lightnin'! What might happen if you're alone and a fit gets the best of ya'?! I won't let you out of my sight," Beverly said.

"It's not my fault!" Isla responded. "It's not like I choose to seize up and shake and drool and everything nasty."

"I never said it was!" her mother said defensively. "But your voice changes, baby. You don't sound like yourself. What might people think if you're in town alone and start speaking in strange tongues? It's hard enough as is for womenfolk here, you'd make it doubly hard on yourself if you give people fodder to start gossipin'."

"I don't care what people talk about! Especially people who can't see what real sickness looks like without thinking it's some kind of trick or spirit or charity," Isla said.

"It matters because when people like that start talkin' it can lead to trouble that we can't control. What if pushy folks wanna send you away? We gotta get what handle on it we can to keep you safe darlin'!" Beverly argued.

"Nothing makes it safe, mama!" Isla scolded. "I'm the one who has to live in this snared body! This fever takes me when it wants. And I have to live in it. Every time! Nothing stops it. And that includes worrying. Fretting isn't worth what good days I've got."

"Just wait until Saturday morn'," Beverly bargained. "We can stop by the bakers and then get some sour spring berries at the market. Do you remember how much you loved those when you were little? We'll visit the garden club to knit with the ladies and chat over tea, then we can spend as long as you want at the library. You've always loved it there. What do you say, dear?"

"Bringing me into the world isn't about you! It's about me! It's supposed to be about my life. Not your life with me in it. Being who you are *for me* isn't enough! I need you to be who you are while *I choose* what kind of person I become.

"You have to let me outside—into town—into peoples' lives. Into whatever hurts, because hurts live here at home too. Don't tell me they don't. Don't tell me that lie too, mama. There isn't anything out there that can be more true than what my bad days in here feel like! My life deserves days where I feel well enough to live them. Why can't you let them be your good days, too?"

"Mamas worry, darlin'. I don't know what to tell you. You'll understand one day," Beverly explained away.

"Being a mama doesn't mean you stop needing to be your own person. That Eli you married for money might think there's nothing more for you than being a wife. But I'm not that small! And I won't let you believe there's nothing more for you than being a mama to a girl that's sick and gonna spoil away," Isla said firmly.

"Don't say that," Beverly whimpered. "I'm just tryin' to do what's best for us. You're gonna get better—you'll see. I talked to Eli and he's gonna fetch you one of them spiritualists doctors folks been talking 'bout to fix your head right up. You'll see."

"Mama, you know that's just fast-talking people taking advantage of folks. You heard what the doc said when I first started shaking. There's no cure," Isla said.

"No. No. Just not one he knew of," Beverly denied. "It'll work. These special kind of doctors are all in the newspapers these days. It's a real breakthrough for folks. It will be for us, too. You'll see."

"And in the meantime," Isla paused with a snarky smile, "will I see anything else other than my bedroom?"

Beverly felt the flush anger in her cheeks drop low and warm her heart. Isla used to stamp her foot when she smarted off like this.

"What would you have me do? Huh? What am I supposed to do? You know what it's like from losing daddy and your little brother. What am I supposed to do with the thought of losing you too, when you run off again without saying nothin'?" Beverly said, slumped and defeated by the grief a mother accumulates over time.

"Promise me you'll do something nice for yourself," Isla said. "Get those old poetry books down from the attic. The ones you used to read from every night in our old house. Sneak out next to the cellar and roll yourself some tobacco when Eli isn't looking. Lace it with a little bit of mint so it tastes good. What does he know about 'ladylike' anyway? Pick and wreath some pretty daisies in the fresh air."

"Promise me that's what you'll do when I'm not around—And I promise I won't sneak off again without telling you, or without another lady friend in town in case I start shaking. Please mama?" Isla pleaded.

Isla never pouted—it wasn't her way. The look she gave was Beverly's favorite infuriation. It was the look that always bent her will.

"Okay, darlin'," Beverly agreed softly. "Just don't slip away from me again."

* * *

Escher approached the hilltop farmhouse set on collecting the rest of his money from Eli.

What have I got to lose? I'll just say what Eli already believes—that Isla is beyond hope. That he should send her away to that asylum as he'll probably do anyway, just now with another reason to belittle an already beaten Beverly. Whatever that monster is will be locked up and I'll be far, far away.

It's not my land. And it damn sure isn't my Isla. But it can be my money.

The farmhouse door opened before Escher even knocked. Eli must have seen him coming. And like most interactions in which one interlocutor pounces on another, it did not go as well as Escher had hoped.

"What in Christ's fucking name have you done?!" Eli said, his face sweaty and flushed red with outrage.

"Come back to collect the rest of my coin, what else?" Escher replied blankly.

"You pikey prick," Eli swore as if his anger would give him flight. "That goddamn whore's louse is up and out of bed, swaying around like she's in full health."

"Brilliant!" Escher said. "Shall I presume a bonus?"

"You bloody well won't!" Eli screamed. Despite sensing that receiving the rest of the money was an unlikely outcome, Escher reveled in Eli's steaming rage. His amusement was only surpassed by his curiosity over what could have ignited Eli's infantile fit.

"Your dark kind coming around my town, and look what you bring with you. Seems like half the town is dead, no proper priest for a civilized Christian place, and the mayor's taken an infatuation with the psychic bullshit you people peddle. He's even hosting a blasphemous séance tonight. Sacrilege in our town's highest public office!

"And then you dare come into *my* house and make that damned girl a worse problem than before! Her own poor mother won't even leave her room now. Locked and useless with some dusty books she fetched from attic junk. Not even tending to the house. I reckon I can make this town good and like it was—and I'd start by getting rid of your kind that come and go through town like locusts that take all that's ours and hard-earned," Eli said.

"That girl was a dent in a mattress and worse when I got here," Escher said. "Besides, how am I so wrong when I agree with you that she's asylum bound? Sure as those who howl at the moon."

"Then explain how she can do that," Eli said, his fury condensing to a growl and a finger pointing over Escher's left shoulder.

Escher turned and saw a woman unbothered by the company of herself, whistling at a chestnut mare trotting in the field beside her. Her long red hair was down and pinned back with a baby blue ribbon. She held a small wicker basket of fresh linens and lilacs in the crook of her arm.

"You see that girl up and walking around?" Eli said with a snarl. "Every minute she's up and walking around Pathyem pretending to be somebody else is a minute and a bit of gold I've got to spend keeping my reputation where I worked to get it. You're going to talk some sense into that witch Escher, and I don't want to hear a peep from your thieving mouth about coin either. You stop her going into town and making a spectacle of my good name. I need enough time to ready the asylum to shut her in there the second she closes her eyes long enough to sleep."

Escher walked down the few creaky porch steps into the long grass and purpling patches of zoysia.

"Hello again, Isla," Escher said. "Don't you look fiery."

She giggled, the laugh of a child remembering the first time her hazel eyes had stared over ocean waves.

I could have swore Isla's eyes were green, Escher thought.

"You must be the Mister Escher that Isla told me about. Shouldn't you know by now that Isla doesn't hang around here as long as you'd like?" she said, playfully twirling with a ballerina's pirouette grace. "I'm Chloe. Don't worry, Isla let me in."

Escher rolled his eyes into a sideways glance at Eli, his over exaggeration keeping the girl giggling. "Can't imagine why you'd leave," Escher said. "But it seems like you can be just about anybody. How do you manage that?"

"Not me, dumbass. Are you slow or something? Isla's the one who can do that kinda magicy stuff," Chloe said.

Her face fell, momentarily saddened but soft like snow settling into playful beauty. "Sometimes Isla changes because she has no choice. There are spirits in the dark that are stronger than Isla—and definitely stronger than you and me, Mister Escher," Chloe said. But her expression lifted with the present moment. "But sometimes she changes be-cause she lets people in. Like me! And I get a moment out of the dark, back in the beautiful day where I belong. I love her for that. Don't you?" Chloe asked.

"I don't know much about that," Escher said dismissively. "But now, why you? Why'd Isla pick you to bring back?"

"Wouldn't you like to know," Chloe said with a grin that highlighted the laugh lines on Isla's face.

Escher was baffled. *A medium so strong that she's like some kind of fairy-tale changeling. This is incredible!*

"This is preposterous!" Eli broke through. "And a drunk's lot of good you're doing encouraging this delusion, Escher. This has gone on far enough and it's time to be rid of you both."

Escher looked over to see Chloe's reaction, but she had turned her back to both men—not in defiance like Escher first thought, but in gazing at a figure sauntering down the afternoon glow as if she was waiting on the sunrise. It was Zander.

Chloe's countenance embodied the shock of a resuscitated heartbeat.

"You know what the most awesome, sad thing about the afterlife is?" Chloe quietly asked. "There's no horizon. You're not in no up nor down. You just are. It's intoxicating, believe me—but it'll never bring you a sight like this."

"Please, please Isla...Just one more day like this," she whispered into the evening.

"Hi'ya, Isla. It's good to see you out of bed and feeling better," Zander said, approaching the house.

"Hello, Bub," Chloe said, touching the corners of her eyes. "Oh…I forgot how bodies cry when they're happy. But I never forgot you."

"What did you call me?" Zander replied. His relaxed figure straightened to attention at the endearing nickname that he hadn't heard in decades, his wide eyes confused at whether his reaction was out of care or clash.

"It's me, Bub. It's Chloe," she said.

Escher instinctively took a step back the first time he saw Zander's hand form a fist. "Isla, I know you sick and you don't know how to fix it. That ain't your fault. But you for damn sure don't know anything about this, this part'a me, or who you claim to be. My sister done passed away a long time ago. Back when she was still learnin' to read good and before I was workin' this land. Stop this now," Zander said. In that moment his tone struck Escher as less of a sharecropper and more like a constable.

"Oh, Zander, I've missed you big brother," Chloe said, pouncing toward him for a reuniting hug. Zander pushed her away with an outstretched arm that sinuously flexed.

"Stop. Now. I know what you are. I know at worst you're a monster because I run from you this morning. I know at best you're a sick girl who can't help herself. But I know for sure, Isla, that you're not my sister. God rest her soul."

"It's me, Bub. Honest," Chloe said. "I used to sneak the laces off your little boots and try tying long, loopy bows in my hair. And you used to blame me for scaring the goats away when you had to get the fussy ones into the barn at night and I wanted to help. And we got us a collie puppy when—"

"I won't listen to no more!" Zander said. "It ain't true and it ain't decent what you're doing Isla. Now, quit it."

A lie, Escher sensed.

"God! You're still so fucking stubborn!" Chloe yelled as she stomped in a pubescent tantrum. Despite the palpable tension, her outburst made Escher turn away to disguise a laugh. Siblings are comical to loners. He saw Eli standing with his arms crossed in disgust.

"I'm so impossible?" Chloe continued in her fit. "You'd rather die on the horse than in the carriage, like being a hero is somehow less tragic."

She put her head down and drew a long, calming breath. She steadied herself with the sureness of a prairie tree-house.

"You remember the time Mother and Father took us to the sea?" she asked. Zander stepped back, reacting to the kind of fear caused by skepticism.

"I'd stand where the waves would break and punch the water as hard as I could—skinny little arms flailing against a massive ocean," Chloe said, remembering with an innocent smirk.

"The tide would knock me back relentlessly just to trickle onto the shore where you stood there laughing. Probably says something about who I would've grown up to be."

"Some kids die," Zander deadpanned.

"Not that day," Chloe said. "You swam out and punched the expanse right beside me 'til I tuckered myself out."

"That's not how I remember it," Zander said.

A lie, Escher could tell with certainty.

"Memories don't belong to the living," Chloe explained, whispering soft assurance. "You lived the experience, but the memory belongs to me. It's like that for all of us that can't be here no more. Memories are so fleeting and fragile in those delicate heads, did we really think they belonged to us?"

"No. No. No," Zander repeated in defiance. He stumbled over his words, a stutter that beckoned at hopelessness. "You sayin'…Chloe…is you not sick no more?"

"Do you want to know what happens when you die, Bub?" Chloe asked, wrapping Isla's slight hand around his pinky finger.

"You get all our memories," she said, her smile bright and alive.

The siblings embraced.

"Isla!" Eli roared, shattering the moment. "You can fool simpletons, but not the likes of me. Zander, ready our horses and carriage immediately. I'm taking Isla to the asylum this very night if it takes me most of sunrise to sort things out with those zookeepers they call doctors. Escher, go and tell Beverly I know what's best for her and us all. Take whatever she wants to give you for your presence and get the fuck out of my town. Tomorrow night I'll hit the pillow without a bother."

The words that came after rumbled like a tectonic tremor.

"You see that little snap pea field over yonder?" Zander asked Escher, nodding to an acre down the hill.

"It ain't mine, but I plow it n' weed it n' kick away rabbits 'cuz Eli pays me with that little house next to it. And you see that little creek next to them trees? I fish in it on Sundays 'cuz it pays me a little peace of mind on Mondays."

Zander turned toward Eli as if rolling over the blade of a freshly sharpened machete—a monster-slaying gladiator finally given an arena worthy of his might.

"But, you lay a hand on Chloe," Zander said, stepping forward with a finger piercing into Eli's chest, "and you cannot begin to imagine the payment you will have earned—I will rip apart your joins and crackle the bones until they sound like your precious coins falling to the floor."

"She is my sister, as sure as she is protected," Zander said.

"You raving, maniac fools!" Eli erupted. "Leave my house and leave my land, all of you! And I'll burn that shithole shack you call a house to the dirt you till for me Zander. And when I come back for you Isla, I'll be coming with the asylum handlers and their thick tranquilizer needles instead of the mercy I've shown you under my roof!" He stormed away and slammed his heavy front door on the nightfall.

The three outcasts stood quiet—sentient scarecrows amid the fireflies and cicadas.

"I can fight for myself," Chloe huffed.

"No offense, but I'd rather fight with Isla," Zander replied.

"Not to interrupt this merry reunion," Escher said, "but Eli mentioned a séance at the mayor's place tonight. Zander, you chose church earlier. Ain't it my turn to pick where we go lookin' for superstition?"

Three eyes widened, one of Chloe's twitched.

SÉANCE ALIGHT

When I was a boy, I watched the Drabarni charm vipers in front of sultanas and cobras before kings. All while recounting the old myths. The sages received lavish rewards from entranced nobles and scattered across the earth, sifting fortune from the wind and pervading nature with magic. But the further they spread across the lands the more resentment and suspicion against them grew. The Drabarni were soon taming bears with chains and monkeys with cords, lucky if they received the stingy copper coins for which they begged. Soon, they were hunted like birds.

And among them was my father.

My father was not born into this caste. He hailed from the most respected musicians and sitar magicians throughout all our peoples' routes. But his family rejected him because he had not inherited his father's voice and he didn't sound like his brothers. Our music has piercing notes that are difficult to replicate, much less master. It requires a powerful voice to convey our mourning ballads through a disorienting veil of buzzing fiddles and frenetic dancing. Our music relives our diaspora. So the musician who could not sing became a showman and storyteller.

His hair was always matted like he couldn't be bothered to brush it. But he carefully combed and tended a magnificently twirled mustache beneath a large and grotesquely broken nose that had been his father's doing. He wore an ornate silver necklace over a red cravat. His gaudy belt buckle was always polished, and he twirled a fox-head cane on the road and the stage. I don't remember him telling a single tale without his long, curved tobacco pipe dangling from a corner of his mouth. The stories and the cherry-hinted smoke billowed out together one and the same. He'd stolen them all.

Nor was my father considered among our peoples' Paramisaras, the vessels born to memorize epics and preserve the oral tradition that defines our shared history. Cut from this caste too, my father was a persona without a belonging.

My mother was also an outcast, the discharge from a family of healers. She favored mysticism over medicine and would not commit to a lifetime spent learning the family skills. She preferred to trade snake oils instead of tonics. So one night she fled beneath the stars, and under them she gathered and sold to many kingdoms the earth's most forbidden growths. Her hands looked delicate but felt rough. Nimble enough to embroider her beautiful floral and mariposa dresses, strong enough to crush a man's spirit into fine sawdust. And she lived well, because slums can't snare an Aphrodite.

Eventually, the runaway mystic and the wanton charmer crossed paths and shared beds. And before you is me.

So the minstrel and the mystic set off together, spinning big lies and little cursed comforts for spare coins and entrance into caravan camps. I've been told they were happy folk, but they weren't from what I recall. That might just be one of them stories too. While craft guilds sent their apprentices abroad for inspiration, they shunned nomads like us. So my pipe-smoking papa told every tale as if one day his family would believe him, and mi madre mixed a monkey paw curse into every cure she made just to spite her ancestors. It shouldn't be a surprise that they knew no better than to reject me too.

Once I was old enough to notice my neglect, I gravitated to Godfather. I followed his road as soon as my naive head was old enough to carry my legs and my load. I went into the world like pollen on the wind—and I learned a thing or two about reading people real fast. Most people start to figure that anything that grounds you has got to be good for something, until they bound themselves down with everything they've got. But for me, the weary tether between my homeland and I has been fraying my whole life, stretching thin every skill or cradle of hope.

Godfather believed there were always new frontiers to explore. But as he got older he increasingly believed that monsters loomed on every horizon. Though this excited me as his young protégé, I grew to understand his hesitancy toward a new era. He once lived among large and ornate caravans that drew local attention and global adoration. But those who became rich have vilified nomads because it is easier to profit from people's conformity than their wanderlust. And now I find myself entering this spiritualist age—one where people are more willing to believe the outlandish. Where once these beliefs were too impractical and erratic for Godfather to plan cons around, they now offer me the precariousness of both larger payouts and more powerful enemies.

* * *

Muddy patches of snow still hibernated on the edge of the mayor's plantation-like estate. The antebellum portico put off newcomers with the hospitality of a cattle prod. The modern wing was a gaudy addition to the old statehouse. Edison lights, polished-brass accouterments, pumps for heated water; Fresh luxuries for old-money elites purchased with a poor tax. It only matched the rest of the property in its haughtiness.

Waxed black and storybook elegant stagecoaches lined the circumference of the pebbled driveway as three unexpected visitors reached the guarded, arsenic-white front doors on foot.

"I fear the mayor insists that tonight's festivities are invitation only," said the valet at the mansion entrance.

"We're here on behalf of the landowner Mister Eli," Zander said boldly.

"The mayor respects and sends his sincerest well wishes to Master Eli for his patronage," the dutiful doorman said above a stiff, starched collar. "But the mayor is not available for matters of governance until tomorrow morning, and Master Eli will surely understand such a private event requires discretion and formal invitation."

Escher stepped forward and straightened his attire with the tact of an unspoken threat.

"My good man," Escher began in the sly tone of conspiring foxes. "Unlike riches, gossip whispered in the mayor's chambers trickles down these very steps and onto the streets of town."

"No doubt the mayor's halls have heard of the lady behind me," Escher said, his vaudevillian arm presenting Isla's figure from the shadows. "I don't bring you Master Eli's paper invitation, I bring you what lurks behind the veil of this town's respected house."

Escher sensed a bead of sweat forming near the conflicted valet's pulsating temple, and he leaned in toward the man's ear. "Such a subject at tonight's...festivities...would no doubt pique the curiosity of the dubiously reputable medium behind these fancy doors, and perhaps your governor even more."

Escher's perceptive ability quite often allowed him tremendous leverage in a conversation. Much like a master lockpick, he could tell when all that leverage needed was just the simplest push to open whatever needed persuading—be it a lock or a layman. Escher felt for the pocket where he had put the first share of Eli's money that he'd received from Zander at the bluestones that morning. He withdrew roughly half of the sum and pressed it into the doorman's palm. *Curiosity requires buy-in*, he thought, and further imagined the satisfying sound of a solved lock's *click*.

"Your worries are valid—if the mayor finds out that you turned away a spirited guest like this...well, are there really many posts left below doorman?" Escher concluded, the noticeable mass of coin pressed into the valet's cold hand.

"Welcome to Pathyem's Daily Manor," the valet said, turning aside and slipping the money into a fold within his starched jacket. "Proceed to the ballroom upstairs with the prudence with which you arrived. And might I recommend the washroom aside the first-floor kitchen for the gentlemens' odor."

"A fine suggestion," Chloe said, the first to enter the manor with a party-going bounce.

Smoke from premium cigars clung near crystal chandeliers and looked like autumn fog clouding lamplights. Chloe, Zander, and Escher mingled on the party's fringes and observed the carousing over flutes of champagne.

"*Megh.* This is disgusting," Chloe said, sipping the champagne like it was camphor oil.

"This is weak," Zander said, his first glass already empty. "I can't believe it was that easy to get in here."

"I can't take you two anywhere," Escher sighed, his attention turned to the devilishly primmed politician exuberantly bounding up the central staircase a few steps above the crowd. His sharply trimmed black beard pointed at his audience as he tilted back and laughed with the gusto of a Shakespearean villain. The crowd softly applauded as the mayor's mischievous, charcoal-lined eyes surveyed his subjects. He held his champagne aloft and began to speak.

"Exquisite and exclusive guests of my hallowed house this night!" the mayor began. "Cheers to us all!"

The crowd laughed and joined in the frolic of snobbery. Escher felt serenaded by the *polari*—that Cracker Jack-sweet slang of carnival cant coming from the politician's rouge lips. If the mayor had lesser aspirations, he could have filled his pockets and tills at any ring-toss or shooter joint in the traveling fair; but instead, he peddled his entrancing power for politics.

"Tonight! I offer you secrecy, my sanctuary, and the anonymity of crescent moonlight. We are bound together by the reason you all bow your heads at night with private doubts you dare not air in the day. Common people, though honest and grounding for us all, would call us crazy. Mad. Or blasphemous. But not the spiritual adventurers who stand before me tonight. For the lives taken from us into an afterlife *SIMPLETONS* dare tell us we cannot contact, tonight, my dear companions, tonight we harken them back."

A skeleton gaunt and piercingly black-clad figure of a psychic woman began descending the marbled grand staircase from the bedrooms above. Her jaw cut as sharply as the cutlass scar below her left cheek. Black high heels accentuated a thin frame that perpetually shifted in the chemical throws of seduction and belligerence. The unpredictably devilish magician wore copperwork gauntlets and the scent of star anise.

When she reached the mayor's side he courteously bowed and kissed her gloved hands.

"I present to you, guests of my house," the mayor proclaimed with the theatrical enthusiasm of a circus ringmaster, "the esteemed medium, Madam Sonora Solset!"

"In your life, have you ever seen a woman like that?" Zander said in awestruck slackjaw.

"Amenable, especially over dinner or a well-woven tarot card tale. Bit boney—mind ya', I don't judge a man or lady inta' that," Escher said, outside the socializing and spellbound fringes.

"*Ow!*" Escher finished, as Chloe's balled fist recoiled from punching his arm.

The psychic's body, shrouded in black velvet and lace, exuded poise and poison. She brushed past the mesmerized mayor toward the crowd. Her doll-black eyes stared blankly as if into a captivating void before her cracked lips spoke.

"We were wrong, and then we died," Solset began, her Mayan chocolate voice smooth yet biting. "Don't be alarmed, *mis infantes*, there's no way you could have known. Not that you would have listened anyway." She slowly slid her hand across the cheek of a debutante.

"I have communed with the spirits of old. Spoken with elder gods from a time before pyramids and sacrificial lambs. They communicate their ancient knowledge with me, and raise me up among their mystics. They reveal to me that our souls are like stars—born to either collapse upon ourselves and vanish, or—"

Solset raised a gloved hand in the air, silencing the crowd though no one spoke. Her eyes leveled at Escher in the far reaches of the guest hall.

"—*EXPLODE*," she finished, spinning around and grinning at the mayor as the innuendo elicited murmured chuckles in the crowd.

"*AREN'T WE ALL*"—Solset's voice boomed with the soaring shriek of a firework, her audience clinging to her charisma and specter—"descended from a billion years of cosmos? Should it surprise us that our last breath be stardust?"

Her voice lowered as she approached a large, circular table in the middle of the grand hall. Her hushed tone held the weight and whisper of transgression.

"Where does fog dissipate when we stop breathing on an icy window, and where does the stardust go when our bodies turn cold in the ground?"

She pulled a heavy chair. She could have chosen any of them, because the moment she sat, she became the head of the table. Empty places were invitations, but not her equals.

"Join my table if you have a strong enough heart to reach out to your dead," Solset said, extending her arms wide toward the rapt audience. "Be the mischief that murders the status quo, and I'll show you where the mist and the mysteries go."

"*Vamos!*" she roared.

The mayor bound off the stairs with the excitement of the first Christmas a child will remember. "Oh, I do hope you'll indulge me," he said to his guests as he reached for the first chair within an arm's length. "I simply cannot miss such an enticing adventure. We have a few places left for brave volunteers ready to jump into the ether."

"What about you, my dear?" the mayor inquired of the doe-eyed girl who'd been approached by Solset earlier. "Fancy going home with a story and making a few weakhearted old folks look foolish for not joining the table with us?"

The girl smiled and blushed, taking a modest step back into the crowd before the flippant judgment of adolescence sent her bustling toward an open chair through a softly applauding crowd.

Cautious partygoers circled the table like pensive piranhas, offering seats in etiquette to disguise fear. A merchant joined Solset's cohort, then an old maid. A house staffer with a bamboo and shell bracelet. Then a mercury-riddled hatter.

Solset stared over the last remaining seat, a performer seeking who among the crowd most avoided her gaze. A county politician waved at the patrons, making sure to balance his portrayal of selfless volunteer and cavalier adventurer. Solset raised her hand the way a queen might stay an execution and shunned the man.

"Forgive me, mayor," she said. "Even an esteemed psychic like myself so rarely gets the chance to read a gypsy." The crowd murmured as Escher shuffled a little closer to the table, his head down and smirking smile quivering like a hound's snarl.

"I sit at many tables and collect dust like a book not much worth reading. Surely such...esteemed...guests outweigh a little meandering novelty," Escher said, his gait accentuated by a thumb hooked in his pocket.

The mayor, confused at Escher's presence at his party but excitedly insistent to begin Solset's séance, sprang from his chair and offered his hand.

"We haven't had the fortune of meeting yet, good sir, but if the lady Solset insists, please, please, join my table with warmest greetings." He extended his palm to the vacant chair and flirtatiously winked.

Escher would have preferred the role of watchful observer instead of taking a seat at the table—a watchful eye on the exit with hopes of a glimpse at the monster. After all—visiting a zoo to see the tiger is one thing, sharing a cage with it is another.

"What's a gypsy?" Chloe asked Zander. Her new body was as tall as his, but she still stood on the tips of her toes to whisper her question in his ear.

"Don't rightly know," Zander whispered back. "Escher's the only one I ever seen, and he's just kinda a wandering prick. I gather some folk treat him n' his kind different just 'cuz they ain't content in one place."

With Escher seated, Solset clapped her hands. Servants dimmed the lamplights. The flicker of a single candle's dying wick illuminated barely more than silhouettes and gloom. "We begin," Solset said. "You all must put your hands flat on the table and close your eyes. Spirits, they approach slowly and only the still."

It was quiet before the destruction.

"We call to the shard spirits," she said in a hypnotic and low-rumbling chant. "Those displaced from this world and untethered in eternity—we offer sanctuary at this table."

Her voice suddenly raised. "We call out to the withers! Those imploded spirits left to meander through the memories of who they once were. To the ghosts of circumstance and crossed stars—we offer the hands you once held."

"Some in this circle gave our dead distance, some kept them close," Solset said. "Who from the neverwhere wishes to approach my altar?"

Solset hummed, a steady tension before a foghorn blast. With her head down, the performer began prodding the sensitivities of her patrons.

"I sense, I believe it is a man. His voice is soft, sometimes incomplete. A name with an R. Ro...Rue..."

"My Reginald!" The old maid said with an upright startle, then a self-conscious cower at her uncouth outburst. Solset grinned and reached over to softly squeeze her cold and frail hand. Escher knew that look, the pleasure of seeing a con victim fall into a trap you patiently laid.

"I am sensing an aura, a family connection. His image is still unclear, but I do not sense youth. The connection seems more mature," Solset said. "Madam, were you ever married?"

"Yes," the old maid said with more restraint but no less frenzy. "My husband. Is it really my Reginald?"

"I sense illness perhaps. Something sudden. It took his voice," Solset continued prying. Escher glanced at Zander from the corner of his eye, suspecting the town's plague must be common knowledge in the surrounding area by now. *And they think I'm a parlor trick.*

"Mind you all to remain focused on your thoughts quietly," Solset said with a schoolmarm reprimand. "It clouds the channel to the other side."

"The spirit is faint," Solset continued. "He says, he says that your care was a testament to your love. He says, I think, he says that he is in a peaceful place with clean water. No, air. Clean air. That he is, finally recovering from that cursed cough."

The old maid cried softly while Escher judged silently. Chloe again tipped up toward Zander's ear.

"I mean, could have just been a lucky guess, right? Do you think she can really, you know, hear from the dead?" Chloe asked.

"I dunno," Zander replied. "You ever hear anything out there? Some witchy woman, a cowbell, anything?"

"I told you already, I'm *not* Isla. I can't do that stuff," Chloe huffed.

"You'd be a lot more interesting at parties if you could," Zander said, trying to stifle laughter at an inappropriate time. "But I guess comin' back from the dead is a pretty good trick too." He playfully bumped against her shoulder, and the siblings snickered together at the back of the room.

Solset began writhing, reminding Escher of boa constrictors he saw performers exhibit when he was young.

"There is a child in the mist," Solset said. "Hardly more than an infant. It retches and writhes. Who here seeks the child?"

The hatter cleared his throat. Drained of his energy like a heart pulled from its arteries, it was all he could do to acknowledge Solset with a small wave from his scabbed hand. *He's afraid he'll never know if it was his fault or not that his child died,* Escher sensed from the poison-laced hatter. *No. He's afraid he already knows the answer.*

"The image is hazy—like smoke. Come closer to us, girl. No—a boy?" Solset's eyes closed tighter. Her face tensed and her eyes watered. "The heat. The fumes. It's so hard to see through this bloody—*ash!*"

Solset arched her back over the top of her chair until her vertebrae popped. Her guttural screaming like birthing pains, as if Solset was delivering a thousand Aztec warriors each wielding a choir of death whistles. The circle of hands around the table was immediately broken.

"My! Uhm, Madam Solset. Madam Solset! Are you alright?" the mayor said, trying to save face at the party debacle.

Escher could see tattoos peeking out from Solset's high and proper collar. Though not unusual for psychics to protect themselves from fiendish spirits with wards and charms and superstitions, these chiromancer symbols burned themselves into once-smooth skin and spread upward into Solset's cheeks with a brand-iron glow. Illusionists and slight-of-hand cons might have their practical effects to heighten the performative aspect of their craft, but whatever was on display at the séance now was well beyond Solset's control. Black suns and staves began cutting themselves into her tongue. Solset bit her bottom lip until it gushed black blood that turned to tar. Her middle fingers bent for a seductive purpose but snapped backward into compound fractures. Cacti thorns formed a chokehold on her neck and noir prickly poppies spread across the table. Solset writhed upward and clasped one hand over the other as if shackled, her broken fingers disfiguring her hands and forming a hell hound shadow on the wall behind her.

"My! What a fit has taken her! Servant, do help this poor, fevered woman to the chambers upstairs will you?" the mayor said.

The terrified servant approached Solset and pulled at her chair, but it remained rooted to its place. Solset's hand twitched like a clock striking midnight, a frightful force from her open palm sending the servant off her feet and careening into the marble steps with a sickening thud. The mayor stammered, the reaction to many an order with consequences only servants have paid. Escher's brow furrowed while others gasped. *Finally, the real magic is coming to dinner.*

"*Linesss,*" Solset said, the final consonant slipping off her tongue with a rattlesnake's hiss. "*Lies, LINESss.*"

Solset shook her head like a snarling hound. And made a snarling noise too. She fought the mudslide of hellish filth that was enveloping her soul and ripping her vital organs from within. The monster wreaked havoc on her with horrid disfigurement. Lurching convulsions and malignant masses propelled her body to climb upon the table, where she crawled toward Escher with cat-like menace and brothel-like gyration.

The color from Solset's face drained into her reddening eyes. "*A-a-adams apple. Callous. L-l-lines. LIESss,*" Solset stuttered.

"*Gyyypsyyy...*" she strained. Escher was now the only one left at the table. The others had scattered or run. The debutante held the dead servant's hand, frozen in shock to the staircase where she knelt, while the mayor tried to subdue the chaos amid the hatter's manic screams.

Zander stepped in front of Chloe, a hand extended back to feel her behind him as much for comfort as protection.

"*Why the lies-linesss, gypsy?*" Solset said with a slithering tongue. She climbed atop the table and crawled toward him with the severity of a lioness predator. "*You are not old gypsy. So why the linesss?*"

"You mean this?" Escher said, pretending to awaken himself by rubbing his face. "Topographical map of my transgressions or one too many night's hard sleep—take your pick."

Solset's legs swung around in front of her and draped over the table. She leaned in and grabbed Escher's chin, pulling him to her face.

"*Run,*" Solset's real voice choked.

She arched back and thrust her left arm out of socket. Zander recoiled at the sound of popped joints and Chloe's shriek as fire burst from Solset's fingertips. Her outstretched hands began to cauterize and blacken and smell like knuckle. The flame lashed out with whip-like tendrils; flickering firelight that took a form like great boa snakes and wrapped themselves around the young girl and fallen servant. The debutante screamed like an accused witch at an inquisition stake and her golden hair filled the room with the smell of sulfur. Solset's dress was now ablaze. Escher stood back, awestruck by the supernatural spectacle of three melting bodies—Solset, the servant, and the debutante—rising together, wholly replaced by figures of ash. The figures moved toward each other, eroding as individual ghosts and their smoldering embers forming a single, horrific Keroax.

A hand rested on Escher's shoulder and pinched more than it pulled. "I didn't come all this way for a bonfire," Isla's voice said in his ear. He turned to face a jade-eyed woman behind him who seemed somehow composed amid the thrashing and the noise and the room now engulfed in flames. Zander leapt toward them, gasping for air in the smoke-filled room.

"What did you"— *cough* —"Where is Chloe?"— *cough* —"Bring back!" he demanded through wheezing and heaving.

"Sorry boys, the girl's gone for now. Do hate sending her to her room so early, but maybe we should take the monster lady's advice, shall we?" Isla said, eyeing the room for exits.

"*A stronger vessel*," the Keroax said through what remained of Solset's mangled voice, thudding steps in its new form toward Isla. "*One who is strong enough to bring us back all our burned.*"

"They offered me the job first, ya' know," Escher quipped to Isla, their eyes locked on the monster. "Had to turn em' down. Sounded like a woman's work."

"Astute of you to know your place," Isla replied as the group huddled closer to the wall. "Mind fixing the drapes?"

"So forward of you," Escher said. He turned around and ripped the window curtains open. Séance guests scattered around the fountain below and onto the manor lawn to gawk at the mayor's burning majestic.

"No. No, no, no..." Zander said, looking over his shoulder at a bad idea and a sizable drop out the window. The entire height of the ballroom, kitchens, and cellars separated them from the water below.

Isla had been in the fire and the smoke and the hell long enough to see more ashen figures shambling toward them, forging themselves into the growing Keroax as it devoured the mansion and the trapped souls that burned within it. *"Our remains scout the air and feel across the earth beneath your feet,"* the Keroax boasted. *"You will be our instrument of resurrection."*

"Maybe, but I feel like a swim first. I'll let you hurry off and get changed. Bye!" Isla said with a teasing wave. Escher wrapped his arms around Isla and Zander. Isla plugged her nose and covered her mouth, the girlish squeal that followed came from Zander. Escher jumped back against the window as the Keroax released itself into a blue flame aimed to kill them. The flames receded as they fell, shining stars and broken glass glimmering in their view of the night sky that was soon muddled by chilly fountain water.

Zander gasped for air and rushed out of the fountain. Escher laughed and ran his fingers through his drenched hair.

"What happened?" Chloe's juvenile voice returned. "I want to go home."

ENTRAIL BLOOD

A rough hand snatched the oldest oil lamp in a dilapidated barn. Eli struck a match, swore when the flicker extinguished itself, then struck another. He lit a nearly spent wick, one of the few things on the property shorter than his temper. The glass scratched into place to shield the tiny flame, which Eli adjusted into a sun-orange plume to light his way—back out the barn door and down the lower forty.

Contrary to his unilluminated approach to the world around him, Eli hated walking in the dark. He always had, ever since he was a weak boy. By that time his father had foolishly frittered away most of the family fortune. The imbecile had invested in misguided scams and bet on his vices more than trustworthy ventures. If Eli cast a lure into the deep stench of stagnant lake that was his memory, he could remember sunny days when maids and governesses were compelled to dote on him like a child of proper standard. Cleanly, reverently, and softly—like the cotton from which they'd made their money. But his fear of the dark came later, when the family could no longer afford servants—when his poor mother was disrespected to do the cooking and sent Eli out to discard the rubbish in the woods.

Eli looked at the oil lamp, swinging in pace with his steps over black, uneven earth. He thought about the oil lamp he would use as a boy, as ornate as it was impractical, also not suited for the work of discarding rubbish.

He wouldn't admit it then, but young Eli was terrified by the nightly chore. Not just beneath his station, but it was the mist—a heavy fog that would roll in with the moon. The thick cloud consumed light and unsettled Eli more with each little step. This dread always heightened near the gazebo—the church white and rotten wood fixture just past the garden.

Eli's drunkard father would spend late summer nights in the portico rotunda, downing bottles of charcoal-filtered whiskey from sunset until the midnight fog and liquor enveloped him whole. Eli vividly remembered the first time he'd disturbed his father by tripping up the creaky gazebo steps. His father lashed a belt across Eli's face and back, then extinguished his cigarette on the beaten, crying boy's arm. Eli only peeked over the gazebo steps to see his father a few more times after that, incurring the same welts and blood and searing scars until he finally stopped.

Eli made his way to the near edge of his land, lording over Zander's sharecropper hut. *How these animals allow themselves to live in such conditions,* he thought. He began idly sliding his feet through scattered hay, kicking flicks of dried grass near the shanty's only door.

He remembered the boy, standing at the steps of the haunting gazebo, the smell of cheap Ottoman tobacco and whiskey-rich piss clinging to the humid air. This time, he didn't dare approach his father's lair. He knew if he did that the beatings would happen again, and that sometime after his mother would tend his wounds with more care than her own. She would stifle a trembling lip while scolding him—"How many times must I tell you not to bother your father in the bleak evenings?" Eli swore he'd become a man and never let his father beat them again.

Eli crept up the gazebo stairs once more, a high-wire act for even the quietest mouse. He saw his father, forgone glutton and abuser of spirits. It wasn't the first time Eli had seen his father blackout drunk, but it was the first time he used his father's unconsciousness as a chance for revenge. Eli's nostrils tinged over the reeking, bile-green vomit dripping through the floorboard cracks and he gagged. For once, Eli backed away without caution. His worn-out shoes sank into the black dirt and poisoned weeds. For a moment, he felt the suffocating fog begin to lift and his lamplight beam brighter. It dissipated the way a burden is dropped or naive childhood fleets.

Eli repeated the motions from memory, recreating how he slung the cumbersome lamp with the heave of an unharnessed tantrum. The familiar sound of shattered glass and gaudy metal clanging off the white-picket decor. How the air smelled of fuel, and a sun-orange spark became a chorus of chaos and blaze. The dry rot wood had kindled an inferno. *Eli remembered how his father screamed while he burned alive, and recalled the sound as if it were a lullaby.*

This memory was now just a shadow in his eyes, reflecting the glint of a hell-hot fire that razed Zander's home and all he owned.

* * *

They shivered on the walk back toward Zander's home, the type of chill and desperation felt when you think there's only one place left to go.

"What was that back there?" Zander asked Chloe, breaking the silence the way moonlight cut the haze.

"Well Bub, I was kinda hoping you'd tell me instead of sulking and being all pissy," Chloe snapped back. "I'm seeing weird shit at a party and next thing I know I'm soaking wet and spitting up nasty water while the whole damn mansion is on fire. Just how bad did you guys fuck things up?"

"Cut it out, Isla! You know that's not what I'm talking about goddammit," Zander said, tension in his shivers. "What did you do with Chloe in the house? How did you do that? Where did she go? And do you have any idea how bad it comin' your way if you do that again?"

"Do you want me to answer every dumbass question one at a time, or just the fucking obvious ones? *I-am-Chloe. And-I-don't-fucking-know.*"

"I believe her," Escher said. "Isla seems more likely to turn into smoke rings than say she don't know something. Like it's some kind of health condition, or maybe just her disposition."

"She can hear that," Chloe said with a giggle.

"Then she can hear this: Don't do that shit again," Zander said. "You brought my sister back, and for that I'm grateful. But you can't just send her back on a damned whim!"

"Even a fiery, certain death trap whim?" Escher added.

"If everythin' is such a whim to you, smartass—and if everythin' is just kindlin' to the Keroax—then let's just get!" Zander said. "We'll gear up at mine, take a couple of Eli's horses, and beat all the monsters and the sunrise outta' Pathyem!"

"I've left towns quicker over less trouble," Escher replied, thinking about how this time yesterday he was in a peaceful, booze-laden sleep by the bluestones.

"I can't go with you," Chloe said, stopping and looking down at the damp dirt road. Her words rang in Zander's ears like the wobbling thud that determines a coin toss.

"Chloe, you just got back. Now, I can't imagine where you been this whole time—either Heaven or nothin'—but you supposed to be here."

"And what about Isla?" Chloe said. "You think it's fair she lock away her own life just for us? Why not for anybody else who miss somebody? Because that's the case for everyone."

Chloe turned to face Escher. The nomad locked eyes with the medium. He sensed Isla somewhere behind her hazel eyes and felt as though she could see through his mesh soul. They all knew the jagged truth that they couldn't face the monster with Chloe—they needed Isla.

"Besides, just 'cuz something's wrong with her head doesn't mean she turn tail and run from anything," Chloe continued. "The Keroax is out for her—and without her it'll get me and all the rest of us just the same."

Zander's grief gradually broke him down the way water erodes a gorge. Escher didn't need his perception to see how the trauma of Chloe's passing had left Zander so emotionally fragile. Escher felt a twinge of grief and missed Godfather again.

"You know, most nothing that was yours lasted," Zander said to Chloe. "Only thing I done held onto was that little hand mirror you kept on your dresser."

"The little one I used to fix the ribbons in my hair?" Chloe remembered.

"Yeah, you loved that little girly thing," Zander said and tried to laugh. "I kept it 'cuz it reminds me of when we were growin' up together. It reminds me how you was always a bushel of happy all the time. I don't like to look at myself in it. I done got rugged and old and it don't look right me and my dirty hands holdin' a pretty thing. It just always help ground me, and ownin' it kept my place without you still feelin' like home."

"If Isla comes back, how am I supposed to know if you'll ever come back? And how am I supposed to fight this monster if I'm thinkin' 'bout you?" Zander said. "I couldn't protect you from what ailed you. Don't tell me the only way I can protect you now is by letting you go. Not for Isla just to get herself killed by that evil thing."

"If you can't fight the monsters without me, then what was the point of me being here at all?" Chloe said. "There's a lot of empty space out there for us who've passed on, but you oughta see the ghosts when their living kin ask for help. They become the closest thing to gods that we've got. It ain't Valhalla, but it's a damn pretty desperation. And I was worth that much, wasn't I?"

"*Ow!*" Chloe snapped with surprise. Escher had plucked a few wispy strands of Isla's long, ginger hair. He turned to the edge of the path and knelt beside the overgrowth.

"What'd you do that for?" Chloe asked in an annoyed huff. She slapped Escher on the back before recoiling her hand to cover her mouth. She reeled from unexpected nausea at what she saw in Escher's hands.

Black, gelatinously sticky blood covered the tips of Escher's fingers as he rummaged inside the decomposing remains of a rabbit left shredded by a predator.

"'The hell are you doing?" Zander asked, confused as to what possible reason Escher could have for the gory mess.

"Real magic," Escher replied. "*Mas o menos.*"

Escher stood, using the hair to string some tiny bones together. He jammed the sharp side of a fractured femur into the underside of a less-than-fully decomposed skull. An organ liquified beneath his fingernails. Three twiggy rib bones formed a gaudy cross-section. Escher extended the disturbing ornament toward Zander in his left hand as a distraction. With his right, he swiftly ripped a shred of red, plaid cloth from the frayed edge of Zander's sleeve.

"Coulda' killed you to ask?" Zander said, examining the tear.

Escher used the cloth to bind the cross-section of ribs to the skull and bone. "Gotta come by surprise or else it won't work," he answered. "Here. I'll prove it."

With that, Escher swung an open palm through the brush. He briefly winced as Chloe flinched, caught off guard by his sudden outburst. Escher pulled back a scratched hand, several lacerations the width of thorn edges. "Oughta be enough to draw blood," he said with satisfaction. He placed the wicked-looking trinket under his hand and squeezed tightly until a few blood drops trickled below his white knuckles.

Escher muttered an indecipherable incantation and opened his hand toward Chloe, who recoiled at the sight of the mangled and stained totem. "Fine. I'll hang on to this for us then," he said.

"Uhm…what's it supposed to do?" she said, poking the least mangled and blood-stained patch of hair. "And why does nature always have to be so squidgy?"

"And where do you come to know witchy stuff like this?" Zander demanded. "I never heard no rumors of the spiritualist doctors making voodoo."

"*Melalo.* It's a binding of protection, specifically an escape charm," Escher said. "This Keroax creature or haunt or whatever you wanna call it will be none too pleased we've evaded it twice now. This little trinket might trick it into losing interest."

"So it'll kill others first before looking for us?" Zander asked. The skin around his temples tensed, either fighting Escher's plan or the chill.

"That, or the superstitious junk won't do a damned thing," Escher said. He kept to himself that totems like this were considered essential among expert Romani crafters, who used them for protection and to confuse those intent on raiding caravan camps. He knew that items like this were grossly off putting to outsiders because they used grotesque animal parts and looked like the tools of witchcraft. But Romani don't use trinkets for curses, and a bauble like this is barely more than something to ward off an anxious mind. But try telling that to anybody else, even though everybody has some sort of protective superstition—a rabbit's foot in the lowlands, a prayer a day in the planes, or ritual stretching in the highlands.

"Chloe's here because she can't leave Isla. I'm here because I won't leave Chloe. And this fucking monster isn't leaving Pathyem until it grinds us and everyone in it into a conscious pile of dust," Zander honestly blurted. "So what are you and your cheap little tricks here for? Huh? It'll kill you too—that Keroax. Fate comes early every mornin', Escher, and it ain't gonna be dark much longer."

"My tricks aren't cheap because I am the price it took for me to get here," Escher said. "And from here, I'm going to kill the Keroax."

"What's that?" Chloe asked. Just before Escher indulged himself in repeating his answer, he noticed her rising fear toward what she'd been the first to see—a dead cat.

A black stray lay sprawled and gashed in the middle of the dirt road that neared Eli's land. Rigor mortis left the creature's mouth agape, white fangs beaming terror into the darkness. But its eyes shone yellow, the reflection of flames a glint in its hell-portal iris.

Zander sprinted forward, slipping as a heel crushed down on the dead cat's ear. He regained his traction only to stumble into the mud again. The suction of earth mixed with his screams and curses and cries until it coalesced into a crescendo of agony. He crawled as Chloe bent beside him, her efforts to comfort him only added putrid mud to her ruined, spring white dress.

"I'm so sorry, Bub," Chloe said, but not just about the fire. "I wish we had more time."

The glow in Isla's face began to fade, replaced by the dim flicker of shadows reflecting the burning shanty. Her body crumpled and braced itself at the broken sharecropper's feet. Gravelly, seizing noises spewed from the fetal position in which Isla writhed—a hideous cacophony of gurgling, choking sounds that melded with the crackle of arson. Zander saw his home burning—the flames engulfing everything and Chloe's spirit slowly fading beside him. Eli had delivered on his threat.

Escher looked up the hill toward the big, unburned master's house and saw the horse-drawn asylum wagon halting near the steps.

BLOOD TURNS ASH INTO MUD

Isla rose from the ground with strained resolve. Shivering wet, half her face now emerged from viscous mud; her intention to upend the gravity of every last tarot card falling into fate.

"Chloe's gone, and now this," Zander said, his head buried in his muddy hands. He screamed. It was an unbearable sound.

"Zander," Isla said shakily. "I'm sorry about Chloe. I was too little to remember her. But I remember ole Miss Mona watching me for a spell while Mama and Papa went to the funeral down at the river. I remember them talking when they got home about ashes in the wind being too pretty a sight for something so sad."

"It's coming," Isla added, a severe gaze homing on the house. Asylum henchmen were dismounting their wagon and readying shackles.

"I see that," Escher replied. "Your suitors are bringing restraints and everything for you, too. Really sets the mood."

"Bigger problems," Isla said. The two watched a glimmering lamplight approaching the Juliet balcony of the mansion's master bedroom. She began dubiously marching up the hill toward Eli's mansion before turning around to face Escher. And for the first time, somebody matched Escher's ability to know a person's fear—and saw that he dreaded the mundane more than the ghastly Keroax.

"You can hear him in there, can't you?" Isla asked pointedly. "You can hear your Godfather's voice in that Keroax."

"Sometimes. Maybe. I don't know," Escher said, surprised and flustered. He quieted himself for a moment, unsettled in the vulnerability that comes when someone sees that you are grieving. When your instincts are to prevent yourself from appearing weak, but your spirits can't find the strength because they and the person you've lost have left you.

"He made me who I am as much as anybody makes themselves who they want to be. There can't be a kind of loss more raw than what Zander's going through. I'd hold on something hard and hateful to avoid feeling that way. But I'd do near anything to hear my Godfather again, as sure as I'd follow any death wish over living a boring life," Escher answered.

"I get it," Isla said. "Sometimes I hear familiar voices, but they just make me wish I wasn't sick any more."

"You'll understand soon enough," she concluded.

Zander suddenly hurtled toward his burning shack of a home, a foolish run-up as he darted into the black smoke and breath-searing fumes. Escher heard burning shelves collapsing and shattering against the dirt floor. Zander emerged moments later from beneath the straw roof, coughing and clutching Chloe's effeminate hand mirror in his war-ready fist.

Fists and fear often grip each other, and Escher's senses clarified the scene like a desperately needed breeze.

One of Escher's many flaws was that he very rarely used his ability to perceive what anybody feared for anything other than exploitation—to get what he wanted or get what he had the opportunity to take. This was the first time Escher had taken the time and looked through Zander's brokenness. To feel his distinct fear of loss along with him—a fear of losing something more than nostalgia. After losing his baby sister, under the pulp press of a sharecropper's life, his mind turning itself into a noose—Zander was no longer afraid of loss. Or of grief. Or of a hard life.

It was fear of losing how he'd remember this beautiful flutter called life.

Zander swung the mirror's smoke-stained ivory handle toward the smoldering front door. Embers scattered up toward the night sky as their reflections fell with the broken glass. Zander dropped the smashed handle and fell to his knees—coughing, bowing before the fire like an alter of repentance, and reaching for the most whole and jagged fragment of glass. When he clutched it, blood squeezed out of his palm and sizzled on the scorched ground. Asphyxiated with rage, he began sprinting up the hill. He thrust the shattered glass in rhythm with his stride as if stabbing into Eli relentlessly.

Escher followed behind him—humming an ominous beat to the battle unfolding before him—ritualizing the severity of the apocalyptic situation with his Romani language.

* * *

Further up the hill, Eli's satisfied smile resembled a sneer toward the crackling bonfire that had been Zander's shelter. He held his head high to deeply breathe in the woodsmoke and burning straw beneath him. And to watch over Isla, walking toward him with what seemed the solemn acceptance that his decision to commit her to the asylum was best. Brawny men with the decorum of shoreleave pirates descended from black horses wearing asylum-white linens. Knuckledragger intellects with hellhound faces. They readied a straightjacket, shackles, and cat-tail whips.

"The boys'll bark, but don't let that bother you fine professionals," Eli said, nodding his head toward Zander and Escher down the hill. "The scrawny one's broken in enough for work. I'll have it out of your pay if you rough him up bad enough to miss a day. You hear me? But I'll pay you something extra and fine to bust up the foreigner with him—and money no object to me as long as he's bleeding. Then get the girl I sent you here for and be gone," Eli said, lighting a cigar in a bedtime ritual.

Isla trudged up her *Gad-Smane* hill, a static sound crackling in her ear and confusing her balance. Voices began to rise in the back of her mind and stood the hair on the back of her neck. She felt her grip on herself loosen and swirl.

Whenever she neared the Keroax she could feel the monster prying to make her a portal, with more demons than angels tearing at the thin fibers of her ability to channel spirits from the other side—like Chloe. Isla summoned the strength to face Eli, to protect herself physically and the power within her from being twisted by men and monster alike. But the pail she put in her reservoir came back empty. The monster clung to her and the heroine became small.

Thugs are more or less the same with or without their kingpins. The asylum workers in their medical linens approached Isla with the shuffle of cavemen. They might as well have come club-in-hand. The goons overcame her in an unfair fight, the abuse of authority as they contorted her arms into the straightjacket.

Beverly, quiet for so long over her daughter's absence, stepped out onto her bedroom balcony in a threadbare nightgown and heaved her burden into the darkness with convulsing and shrill shrieks.

"Don't take her!" Beverly threatened through an unrelenting torrent of tears. "You can't board up a life just 'cuz you weren't there for it, Eli. She's all I have left of mine, and if you take her away I'll burn your roof to the floor."

You see, the problem with men like Eli isn't that they've got no heart—it's that nothing is real to them until it's got blood on it. To men like Eli, money isn't earned until it's taken out of a weary hand and an animal isn't meat until it's mounted. They want the fights they choose, but they don't want to be challenged—and certainly not in front of their inferiors, which to them is everyone.

And be damned before it comes to taking it from a woman.

"Jesus Christ, woman," Eli muttered through quick puffs of his pungent cigar. He stepped in front of a few chuckling hospital henchmen and took Romeo-like center stage on his front lawn. Another, longer drag from his rich roll of tobacco and he dismissively extended his arms to his sides.

"Now, Bevy," he began, a crooning tone with a disarming sway. "You listen to me. Now we both know you're gonna' do no such thing. You may drive me crazy every now and again woman, but you got a husband that's good to you. And you're a good woman who keeps a real good home. So why would you want to burn all your nice things down for? Then what would you do?

"Now it's bad 'nough you got a girl causing ruckus around here and in town. But my wife should know better—hollering and half dressed on the balcony for a night this cold. Now I've worked everything out, a solution that's nice and quiet and clean like everything that's ours. So put the lantern down Bevy, so you can fetch a coat and come down here. You hear? Isla's all ready to go. She understands. You can say goodbye like a proper mother while the doctors and I get her sorted."

The asylum men heaved Isla's restrained and sick body into the wagon. She began convulsing, another pulsating seizure blasting through her frail frame.

Beverly had heard words like this more or less since she was a growing girl. For a lot of people, last words are wasted or left unsaid—hers just went unheard.

Beverly turned her back to the asylum wagon. She never showed rage like this in front of Isla. Cool air glided over her arms as she slammed the lantern against the doorframe. Glass broke and metal rang as the remnants bounced against the wooden balcony. Her tears fell like exertion sweat, and the flames spread alight the propellant of anger she cast from deep within her. The fire began to grope a cotton-fabric curtain until it engulfed the doorway. She turned and stood in the foreground of a remorseless hellscape, a vesuvian stare toward Eli that might encase him in ash should she blink.

"God! Dammit! Woman!" Eli said in sucker-punch gasps. The cigar that dropped from his hand fell into the mud and extinguished as Eli ran beneath the balcony. "Why would you trap yourself out there like that Bevy?"

Beverly closed her eyes. Finally, she couldn't hear the expletives and lies she hadn't been able to drown out for most of her life. She found stillness in the hypnotic crackle of the arson behind her.

"Jump Bevy! Jump! Christ, jump!" Eli screamed and gestured with his open arms in a carnival barker's frenzy.

Beverly turned back to see the fire, captivated by the kaleidoscopic hues of unleashed heat. Black smoke dripped into her lungs as she inhaled deeply, like she was being smothered by dark waters. To her, it smelled like the fireplace that warmed the cozy sitting room where she used to play with young Isla. And that's the dream she clung to until she collapsed.

"Bevy—no!" Eli croaked through the rising pain in his dry throat. "I'll bring you down! You just wait." The flames cascaded down the staircase and extracted sap from the once exquisite banister. Eli lunged across the threshold he'd once carried Beverly over years ago. He died with everything around him on fire.

A few moments later, Zander's madman sprint stopped just short of the front door's fiery fumes and blinding flickers. He did not reach the house in time to have his revenge on Eli. Zander's furious yell eclipsed even a regretful suicide's life-clinging shriek. He threw the jagged mirror glass against the blazing house. The tiny debris made no noise and added no more than a speck of ruin to the engulfing destruction.

Escher was the last to arrive at the burning house. He lagged behind the spectacle because he didn't make a habit of volunteering for losing fights. And the raging fire and its lineup of four hulking hospital goons certainly looked to be a losing fight. Zander, however, measured fights by his thirst for one. He had wanted to kill Eli, and the inferno had taken that chance from him. When somebody like Zander doesn't get the fight they need, they'll take the fight anybody's willing to offer.

"Nobody. Nobody is taking anything, or anyone else, away from me again," Zander said. It was the line he drew as a border to leave what pained him behind. With Zander's fists flailing forward, the sound of crushing bone and bruising flesh ensued between him and the asylum men. Escher slipped past the distraction and kicked at the wagon door until the latch gave way. He helped Isla out of the jacket. Her gentle hand—cold as a corpse—slipped into Escher's palm. He expected a hurried tug, the pull of Isla's flightrisk escape.

But this was the grip of two hands with little else to hold onto before reckoning rains down.

Who wouldn't have expected tears from Isla? But no. She was wide-eyed. Terror tends to strike before grief leaves its lingering rumble. The fire now licked the front porch steps, which oozed black atrophy like a wound. Beverly had turned the house into her own incinerator and Eli had burned alive in his own mausoleum. The smoke billowed many stories over the collapsing home, and from it rose the grand Keroax it had ominously promised to be.

WHERE THE MIST GOES

Escher pivoted to see Zander huddled on the ground, flinching in self preservation as two asylum men kicked his head and gut. Two other men lay bleeding from broken noses and caressing bruised ribs, crawling toward their panicking wagon horses. The asylum men had numbed themselves to many evils and dehumanized many lives behind bars and in unlit halls.

But the Keroax that had risen from Eli's house dwarfed them. The men over Zander backed away quickly, one tripping over Zander's surely broken leg. The other goon lifted his thug comrade by the belt and slung him into the back of the wagon. The two slammed closed the cage that had been intended for Isla while the other two henchmen lurched themselves off the ground and mounted the reins, which they lashed in a panicking whip.

The Keroax arched, tearing the house apart in a burning cascade of ruin. Its titan-like arms burst through the walls and smashed into the earth with a dreadful quake. The hell-born monster's right fist enveloped the escaping wagon and ground the asylum henchmen into dust so faint it would never be seen in a sunbeam. This gave the Keroax a lustful pleasure as it engorged itself on more conquered souls. The monster leaned toward Isla and Escher, who embraced against its duststorm of dying breaths. For a moment, the scene stood as still as regret and silent as a heartbeat that can no longer be found.

Escher stepped forward. He balanced on his left foot and began to pivot, drawing a crude circle in the soot-covered ground with his right heel. Isla watched Escher's uncoordinated shuffle around her as if it were a carefree dance in the rain and not the ash that fell like snow. He backed away for a moment to admire the imperfect circle he'd made with his boot—the path over his own little globe—before approaching the Keroax.

"You see this little patch of dirt, clear of your reeking dust?" Escher said with disinterest in the monster's answer. "Seriously, do you not ever wash up or brush yourself off for someone special?" He turned and winked at Isla.

The Keroax pulled itself up taller, reveling in Escher's challenge the same way it fed off the heat that ravaged Eli and Beverly's remains. It shrugged with the disquieting rumble of a settling house.

"Inside this circle is the safe world—everything from morning coffee to workin' days and bedtime stories," Escher began to explain. "Now, the church might say all of this is under their protection for just a little patronage and alms in priests' palms. That peace comes with a god in the home and on the throne. But you and I, monster, we know better than that don't we?"

The Keroax snorted with a force that spewed broken window glass. Its shrapnel cut Escher's cheek, which he wiped away a trickle of blood and carried on.

"Ah, you've gotten used to hearing unanswered prayers while playing with your prey, haven't you? Nah, nah, nah, you'll hear no god or king's name from me," Escher said. He nodded toward the ground. "I've crossed too much of this little scorched earth for that. And it looks like I've reached the edge."

Escher stepped forward to the high-noon rim of the circle, Isla in the safe world behind him.

"The world is scared of people on the fringe, thinking only the devil could be behind them. They don't even know what to call us, other than 'nuisance' and 'torment' and 'gypsy.' But my tongue is much older than these babblings. We call ourselves '*Cikani*.'"

The Keroax recoiled in recognition of a worthy enemy.

"We are the foreigners, heretics, and gyptian black magicians who keep the devil in the dark. We take the names used to curse us and give them to our most valiant. And I am Escher." He stepped outside the circle. "And the truth about those of us on the fringe is that you can't repel the monsters without frightening the faithful."

The Keroax flinched and burst forward, encasing Escher's torso in a crushing fist. Isla shrieked with a wraith's ear-rupturing pitch as the Keroax lifted Escher high into the air. He felt a crunch in his ribs and spit blood with a wet, retching heave. His fists clenched and he felt the ripple of cracking bones. He ground his teeth and exerted everything within himself to stretch out his hand amid the volcanic tornado of the Keroax. In it he held the gory totem he'd made on the road back from the séance.

The totem flickered like a fleeting star and its brightness stunned the Keroax, which dropped Escher and his now broken protection to the hard ground. Escher lay flat against the earth. Not peacefully placed like a corpse laid to rest, but not writhing either. Just the stillness that accepts surrender.

Smashed to death by a demon—not the worst way to go, I suppose. Better than choking on shoddy stew or drowning in stagnant water. Can't be long now, Escher thought. At least now he would lose his life to something truly breathtaking.

He very nearly closed his eyes—syrupy darkness blanking his periphery—when he saw Isla's muddy shoes. She stooped and gathered the broken remains of the flawed totem that had been meant to protect them. She stroked Escher's cheek with the back of her hand as he felt a pull on the back of his aching neck. Something shimmered in her hand as she backed away, her smile dissipating into a memory that would never leave him—her poise extending pity before inflicting incomparable pain. He lurched upward, shakily steadied himself on his forearm, and clutched at his chest where his godfather's pennant once swayed. If it had been Chloe, then maybe the girl would have listened to him urging her to run away. But not Isla.

She took the delicate, pale gold chain and used the glittering metal to bind Escher's totem stronger than before.

She knew more about his mystic ways than she had let on. But by the time he realized how much she truly understood about him, his heart could only wrench his throat to plea "No." He'd seen Isla fend off sickness and seizing tremors, but there's not enough gold or exotic magic in this world to fend off death.

But Isla's world could.

"Cunning is just amateur magic," Isla said. "Let me tell you about some real magic, Escher. Ancestors are our best protection, so I'm bringing them all back. Just try to remember me and what happens next as something more than a curse."

Isla hummed. Escher would find comfort in her tune long after the moment that changed him. It fluttered like the whistle of a sweet breeze through a crackling fireplace and landed on the ear as softly as overdue love. Escher and Isla orbited each other's gaze—twin stars spinning amid a supernova's blast – when the Keroax swept her high into the air.

The manananggal monstrosity beamed a devilish grin of billowing white smoke. At last, it held the conduit it needed to wake the world to a nightmare.

Isla's hand clung to Escher's amulet, tenaciously holding the devil in hell. She felt the monster enveloping her from the inside. She had little time left to wield her ability to channel spirits and precious little breath to waste.

"I can hear the voices inside you. Empathy is the closest we can get to death. And if that don't terrify you, then it's too late," Isla told the Keroax, hoarse from its crushing fist.

"Even for the monsters," was the last thing she said.

Isla's spindly thin fingers wrapped around the mended amulet. She plunged her arm into the ashen monster and screamed with a piercing warcry. A bright flash crackled from the amulet and cast itself throughout the Keroax, a cherry-blossom hue ripping through the smoggy colossus. The looming figure of the Keroax began to settle back onto the ground. It lurched as smoke spread across the earth like unearthed roots. The monster knelt, and an aurora light as vibrant as a spring sakura bled over its fist that lifted Isla high into the air. Escher lost sight of Isla, as her body floated into the type of clouds that hammock themselves in a raging volcano. The monster's ash and ember consumed the amulet, and the Keroax weakened to mere mist. It thrashed and shrieked at a pitch of worn brakes on metal. The Keroax tore at its midsection, a wound splitting the monster in half like daylight breaking a horizon. Smoke poured from the gash, and a gale leveled what little remained of the house and roared over Escher.

He couldn't escape the billowing plume that engulfed him. For a moment, Escher smelled the sulfuric stench of his singed hair. Then he couldn't smell anything at all. The asphyxiation navigated deep into his lungs and buckled his knees. Escher coughed. His eyes watered, then parched. Blood pooled in his tear ducts and the phlegm in his trachea turned to tar. He felt his balance spin and his heart seize.

But he did not die. In that moment, Escher began to understand how Isla had saved Pathyem but condemned him. Whatever groundwater soul Escher had in this moment began to well up and overflow. Through the dissipating smoke of the vanquished Keroax, Escher absorbed all the souls Isla had cast out of the monster and into the Romani.

The soul of every person to ever die and be dedicated to cremating fire had found sanctuary in a vagrant.

THE CLIFF

I would go on to tell the story no more times than I had to. But the first time I recounted tonight's events sounded more or less like this.

The Keroax was a beast of narcissism. It ripped consciousness from cremated souls and sought to use them to raise the buried and decayed. All it wanted was to show the world its grandiose rot. Isla, the most cursed portal in Pathyem, could channel spirits from the afterlife and fleetingly return our most cherished departed—like she had with Chloe. But the presence of the Keroax was too strong for her because channels are not meant to be vessels, the same way a tap is not a cup. So she mended Godfather's amulet, combining the superstitious and the sacred to channel the hostage souls from the Keroax into me. In doing so, Isla absorbed the monstrous Keroax and sacrificed them both into oblivion.

** * **

Escher laughed, a panicked and psychotic chuckle. "How? It's not possible. I can't still be here!"

Escher struggled to his knees, coughing up thick and sticky blood. He balanced himself with a hand on the ground, the other dusty hand wiping his mouth. "Why am I still alive?" he yelled into the darkness over the smoldering rubble of the house. The bodies of Zander and Isla lay still like scattered debris. The mess of everything lost strewn about like Escher's own reckless life.

He screamed again, this time in pain. A calamity of voices shrieked in his head, crippling him as he felt his skull would erupt. "Why am I still here then, aye?" he screamed, staggering to his feet and wailing in newborn anguish.

Escher willed himself to the property's highest point, a limestone cliff that overlooked Pathyem the way Eli had looked down on everyone. Escher believed the sight was probably one to behold if it weren't for the darkness of night and what had become of him and his—dare he say it—friends. Escher shambled to where the grass draped over the cliff. Moonlight-blue nightshade blades fluttered in the cool breeze, coaxing Escher over the precipitous drop. The first of many tears began to fall from Escher's face. At first they were his tears, then the spirits added theirs. Their salt stung his singed wounds and cascaded over the malham gorge.

"Come on, come on..." Escher repeated in a whisper, gently rocking heel to grass-bent edge.

What makes an end as bearable as any other?

"Come on."

What difference does it make not to?

"Come on!" Escher yelled in a pitch that would slander blasphemy. The voices in Escher's head went silent in the way that crystals bind snowflakes, as if what made Escher broken—his buried grief over Godfather, his parents' abandonment, his estrangement from community—might somehow be bound together again; that Escher could be made whole by the multitude of spirits he'd absorbed through Isla's sacrifice.

Let bleakness come meekly.

And with that thought, Escher lunged off the cliff—one last flit of courage spent on suicidal cowardice.

He felt the air rush around his body, weightless as a dream and plunging as sin. He swore ever since the fall that he heard buskers, smelled Godfather's pipe tobacco, and felt the thud of flesh on sharp rock.

So much blood, it would have been a horror for even a butcher. It spewed from his body like a pomegranate being pulped by a machete. Like an extinguished candle, darkness absorbed Escher instantly. But a mysterious smoke lingered over the haunting, resistant to join the wind. The smoke rushed back into Escher's broken body, and the ashen spirits within began to restore him—returning him to look more or less the same as he had before the death-lusting plunge. Some of the more forthright spirits attempted to cameo how they had once appeared in life amid the mystical resurrection.

Escher's eyes slowly blinked open. He had no set belief in an afterlife, but he doubted it looked like Pathyem from this angle. "How...am I still here?!" he shouted.

He lifted himself from the blood-covered moss and looked up at the cliff high above him. Flush with anger, disappointment, guilt, and a smattering of blood, he trudged around the chalky-white rock face and back toward the same edge from which he'd lunged. Back atop the peak of Eli's land, Escher repeated the gruesome avalanche of flesh and blood and brains shattering on the ground below. The souls of cremated spirits channeled through his crippled body like steam releasing off a mighty engine. And again, the spirits restored his body from the inside out. And again, a Sisyphus trudge back atop the cliff. And again, the smashing against rock. And again, ashen souls mending all that had been broken inside him. Over and over, bones snapped like branches in a gale and muddy footprints pooled with blood. Over and over, busker spirits sang in Escher's coma and billowed smoke until he was whole again.

Once again atop the cliff, Escher saw the daybreak pink of sunrise. This time, Escher sat on the trampled ledge, legs dangling over where he'd fallen so many times. As the sun rose over Pathyem, Escher said, "It seems I've run out of darkness."

* * *

A few hours later, the sunrise fully lit the eastern field where Zander's house lay in blackened rubble. Tiny puffs of smoke danced on the spring breeze that dried morning dew as if wiping away last night's tears. Zander sorely raised himself off the ground, brushing away the ash and grimacing at the wounds to remind himself he'd survived. He saw Escher nearby, sitting at the crest of the cliff overlooking Pathyem and the river that washed away drifting ash.

Zander saw Isla's limp body lying on its side. He hobbled to her, unable to bear the weight of another traumatic death. With his injuries he had never needed help so much in his life, but seeing this death marooned Zander like a shipwreck being pulled to black depths. He rolled Isla's body over to check for any sign of life. A weak voice peeked through the early morning birdsong like a fledgling prayer.

"Bub? Are you okay?" Chloe said.

LEGION UNLEASHED

"So, you're tellin' me Isla figure out some way to take that monster out with her and leave that girl Chloe a body so she could come back to life?" Darby asked.

"Pretty much," Escher answered. "Best I can tell anyway. Back when I first saw that monster get a real hold on Isla, it's like she could actually *be* people from the other side. I mean, really bring spirits back the way she did with Chloe there for a while. She could hear all these voices that I can hear now. And there's so many of them, Darby. So, many. And Isla brought one of them back to life! Chloe's voice is alive now. It's impossible, and yet she's right back there on the hill where Isla left her.

"But it don't feel like that with me. All these spirits don't well up inside of me the same way that one could with Isla. Seeing what Isla did to bring one person back will keep me whole for the rest of time. And that's, well that's breathtaking."

Escher took another bite of stale biscuit and fresh eggs at the bar. He'd retreated back to the tavern and knocked on Darby's door for a purgatory minute until she gave in and cooked him some breakfast in exchange for a damn good explanation. And he'd tried his best to give her one.

"How the hell you still standing, boy?" Darby said with incredulous curiosity, she could have sworn his green eyes were a different color when she'd first met him. "You gotta be more spent than a workin' girl outta tricks. You reckon you some fairy tale hero who never gon' die now?"

"I don't think so," Escher answered. "I think I just got full of souls from cremated folks, not buried ones. The Keroax monster didn't have them. He wanted Isla's power for that. But we've been cremating folk for a long time. I don't even have to look far to know that's a lot of years."

"That's no shame. We most human when we feeling for other people. It ain't just conscience in yer' heart, it's what you let yourself live through. And it sure looks like you're in for a lot of livin' now," Darby said.

"I can hear them you know," Escher said, as if there was any way the bartendress could know what he was talking about. But she was used to people sitting at her bar thinking she could read their thoughts. "The clans I come from, there ain't much to indicate help will come from outside the caravans we spread over many roads. Extended family is usually the only home we remember, and they almost always get ripped apart like my kin. But when Isla slayed that legion monster, she left me a family to take on the road. And I suppose they have a defender now."

Escher sipped his lukewarm coffee from a beer-stained mug. Darby's hired help hadn't come in to wash up yet.

"I don't know who or what I am anymore. I know so many things I never knew how to do before. I ain't never worked a harbor, but I got a soul somewhere in these hands that can tie a dozen maritime knots. I got other folks' memories that can lift me up or drop me off a cliff. I can hear their voices. And of all the languages I can speak now, not a one of 'em will shut them up," Escher confessed. "I gotta find a way to make it better. And it sure seems like the only way is to find out who I am from now on."

The bartendress nodded. In their two conversations, it was the first time she'd really listened.

"Every day we wake up, we face a new world, boy—whether we like it or not. We alter our world and our lives to face each day. You gotta live long enough to see what works; to throw away what don't work; and to stop being pig-headed about it all," Darby said. "And well, at least ya' got company this time."

Escher snorted on the last of his coffee and felt the coarse grounds in his sore throat. They laughed together at the absurdity—because absurdity is sometimes just the thing you need to find in sadness.

"You know, I thought if I just listened hard enough, that maybe if I just sat still in the sun this morning and looked over the river that runs through town, I might be able to figure out what that drunk told you before he drowned. I thought it might make a good parlor trick," Escher said.

"They didn't burn him," Darby explained. "He wash up close to the church, so the ole' priest back then bury him in they yard. Good Catholic resting and all. They don't burn em', so I guess you can't hear him. But I reckon you best get outta town before word spread about them fires and the town go blamin' it all on a gypsy."

Escher stood from the table, thanked her for the breakfast, and placed his last few coins on the bar. Darby swept them into her hand and wiped things down with a dry rag as he walked to the door.

Escher turned before leaving the tavern. So much had changed since he entered this bar just two days ago. Maybe his path would lead him back through Pathyem someday, maybe the road full of souls would wear him down altogether. So just in case...

"What did he tell you? Before he went under water," Escher asked Darby.

"Don't tell 'em I couldn't swim," the Pathyem bartendress said.

* * *

Escher drove. Fools-gold gilded wheels accelerated toward the sunrise—a sleek, inline wagon with galloping horses bearing east.

He'd pieced the stretched canvas caravan together over the past few years on the road, weeding out the voices in his head to pull aside a few dozen old-hand carpenters and a couple recently cremated engineers. The voices of a few electricians and scientists chimed in until Escher gave one of the gear-head mechanics—a twangy voice called "Little Bob"—right-of-way to shut em' all up. With Little Bob the freshly appointed foreman and Escher as the hands, they assembled a caravan the likes of which was not seen until Kettering's electric decades later. This morning, he had dismissed the voices of Little Bob and his team of builders in favor of the sound of wind and miles left behind.

But Escher knew he had poured so much effort into this meticulously crafted chariot for two, intrinsically specific reasons.

Having a project is good for everybody. Something to keep the head and the hands and the heart engaged. Something to mull each night as fatigue ferments into sleep. This is especially important when you can't figure out a way to die.

Also, and despite the clamor of the many mechanics in his head, Escher had little interest in maintenance. He dealt with enough of that as is inside his own body. Why, there wasn't a doctor anywhere a bird would land who'd believe what Escher had been through.

Ever since the incident with Isla—rest her soul—he'd consulted a rolodex-worth of doctors among the voices in his head, witch healers and school-credited medics alike. Even if he'd bothered to keep track, he still would have lost count by now of how many times he'd fallen ill and expelled ash or smoke or crumbled embers from every orifice. Best he could reckon: a new heart formed in his chest every decade or so, kidneys thereabouts the same. Lungs came and went like a cook goes through potato peels. Livers regenerated at his own moderation and peril, usually about every six months. An occasional glance in the mirror came with a pleasant realization that his skin had become a little more taut and evened out his old age, just the jolt he needed to get out of bed with a few less creaky joints and sore muscles. And though his eyes occasionally shifted their hue, they always told the correct time of how long he'd been cast to wander.

Whenever he glimpsed another unsettling defect, Escher typically consulted the voice of that old doc from Pathyem who'd died of cough before the Keroax emerged so long ago—at least three hearts ago by now—because of the doctor's genial bedside manner and liberal permission for bloodletting. Escher would take razors to his wrists until he succumbed to sleep—a poor night's rest, smooth arms, and a bloody mess awaiting him each inevitable morning. Each time he awoke came an ear-splitting screech of last gasps from souls that had burned during his slumber, and he'd hush the frantic bardo that Isla had built in his head until the cacophony of pain was once again a quiet catacomb. Then he'd make coffee.

Escher set himself upon the prospect of his next con as if it were a velvet stanchion ushering him into a gilded age.

Since the Keroax and the *incident of souls* as he'd come to think of it, Escher had gathered an eclectic conglomerate of thieves, dirty dealers, and mentalists proficient in both illusion and sleight of hand. Consulting the less-reputable voices among his multitudes only extrapolated the joy he took in trickster thievery—his first terminal condition.

* * *

There is a place beyond loss. Where nomads follow the lights of distant piers that flicker on the edge of evening. Where Spanish moss shades the path to front porches and fog rolls off amber mountains into gray skies that never rain. Where we are guided through lush forests by the hands we choose to hold. Where we find deep sleep on desert nights beneath the stars of Zagoran skies. Where cobblestone streets lay out before us like cavernous adventures, and friends gather over oil and plenty. Where bread doesn't touch the ground, but sits on gates and low walls in abundance for none in need. There you will find me and my ghosts, leaving campfire cinders and star-crossed faults behind.

THE END

Author's Notes

I began writing this book shortly after hearing about the story of Lurancy Vennum, the "Watseka Wonder" from Illinois in the late 1800s.

This book is also about a pair of siblings I knew long ago, who grappled with the worst gut-punch that mortality has with which to split us apart.

Vennum was a teenage girl afflicted with epileptic seizures that led to extended periods of unconsciousness. Upon awakening, Vennum would claim that she had visited heaven during these comas and communicated with angels and deceased siblings. In addition to copious bloodletting, doctors recommended that the Vennum family should send Lurancy to an asylum; however, the desperate family tried one last-ditch effort. The Vennums' neighbors, the Roff family, were spiritualists—a vibrant and voguish belief at the time that popularized séances and contact with spirits. The Roff family called in a spiritualist doctor, E. Winchester Stevens, to assess Lurancy's condition. Stevens claimed many paranormal incidents occurred, including instances where Vennum read an unopened letter and channeled people similar to those portrayed in this book. After a particularly nasty seizure, Vennum awoke from a coma and claimed to be none other than Mary Roff—the neighboring family's deceased daughter. Roff allegedly inhabited Vennum's body for several months, including living with "her" family in the Roff's home. After a series of farewells, Mary Roff changed back to Lurancy Vennum—who reportedly never experienced another seizure for the rest of her long and fulfilled life.

This book is also my attempt—in the absolute smallest of tributes—to bring Chloe back, even if just for a fleeting time while you read this.

Aaron Mahnkey's podcast series *Lore* contains the most clear summary of the "Watseka Wonder" story that I have encountered. Episode 50, titled "Mary, Mary," was released in December 2016. Another episode, "Carried Away" released in April 2018, was also informative regarding how popular culture often misrepresents Romani "curses."

Which leads us to by far the most problematic subject matter in this book, Romani culture and language. Many of the details surrounding Escher and Romani life were directly adapted from literature and exhibits in the Museum of Romani Culture in Brno, Czech Republic. Since this is not my life experience, it is not possible for me to represent the Romani diaspora with any degree of accuracy or inclusion. That is why Escher's background specifically draws from this one region of Romani life, including pejorative statements and racial slurs aimed at Escher that are direct quotes from this source material.

About the Author

Jim Stallings is an English teacher and journalist who has traveled through nearly 40 countries. He infuses many of the wonderous people and places he's visited into his supernatural thriller, *All The Futures That Never Happened.*

EXPLORE NEW HORIZONS
WITH US AS WE SAIL ONTO
SHORES OF LATEST
PRODUCTS, EVENTS, GREAT
TITLES, AND BEYOND.

VISIT US:
WWW.OCEANIACOM.COM

OCEANIACOM PRESS